TIPPERARY
FOLK
TALES

TIPPERARY
FOLK
TALES

AIDEEN MCBRIDE

The
History
Press
Ireland

First published 2015

The History Press Ireland
50 City Quay
Dublin 2
Ireland
www.thehistorypress.ie

British Library Cataloguing in Publication Data.
A catalogue record for this book is available from the British Library.

ISBN 978 1 84588 849 7

Typesetting and origination by The History Press

CONTENTS

ACKNOWLEDGEMENTS

My thanks to the following for whose time, help, guidance and encouragement I am deeply grateful: my family – David, Ellen, Michael and Sarah McBride, Nicola and Laura Moore and David and Mark Sheehan; Críostóir Mac Cárthaigh and the staff of the Folklore Archives UCD; the staff of the National Library of Ireland, Kildare Street; Tom Whyte; Terry Cunningham; and fellow folk tale authors Richard Marsh, Steve Lally, Brendan Nolan, Joe Brennan, Anne Farrell and Nuala Hayes.

INTRODUCTION

In 2013, my father and I were invited to write the Carlow edition for The History Press Ireland's folk tales series. It was a very enjoyable experience, delving into local histories, discovering yarns and tales of local places and people, and learning new things about my county. I so enjoyed the results of those hours of research and discovery that afterwards I approached The History Press Ireland to see if there were any other counties still in need of an author in order to complete the planned series. My nearest neighbours were already in the process of being written but Tipperary, I was told, was still in need of an author. So, after a few initial enquiries, I took it on.

I am not a native of Tipperary, which I felt put me at a disadvantage. As a child, I had visited some of the well-known sites in the county; the Rock of Cashel, Cahir Castle and Holy Cross Abbey, but other than that I was not overly familiar with its geography or history.

This project has changed all that. I had to leave the motorway and main roads and take to the back roads, in a journey both physical and literary, to bring together this selection of stories and lore. What more enjoyable way can there be to learn about a place than to delve through its histories and stories? No more will I take the motorway to quicken my journey to another destination.

Tipperary has become for me a destination in its own right, somewhere that, of a summer's day, I can load the car with a picnic and say, 'Come along and I'll show you where …'. I hope that this book might have a similar effect on those of you unfamiliar with the county, that you too might be inspired to take the chance to visit a place steeped in history and folklore, and maybe discover some of those hidden places for yourselves.

To the natives of Tipperary, I am sorry I couldn't tell every story. There were so many and not enough pages, and I know even now I haven't heard them all yet. I hope this short selection goes some way towards supporting your pride for your county. And why not be proud? Tipperary is a county linked with the very beginnings of Ireland. The very first entry in the *Annals of the Four Masters* refers to the arrival of Cessair and her companions on the shores of Ireland, and her coming is linked to Tountinna in the Arra Mountains. Tipperary is a county that has seen its share of suffering; under the Danes and Vikings, under Cromwell, and through the famine. Yet, it has stories of hope, resourcefulness and determination throughout. It is a county which stood against the tyranny of unfair landlords and produced leaders who toiled for Irish freedom. It is a county of saints and kings, of wit and wonder.

This book is just a selection of the stories from across the county. There are places like Cashel, the Glen of Aherlow, and Slievenamon so steeped in Irish mythology and history that you could fill a book on them alone. Indeed others have, and in my searches I have come across *My Clonmel Scrapbook*, a 380-page volume by James White, first published in 1907, with stories and newspaper clippings of Clonmel, and John O'Neill's *Handerahan the Irish Fairyman and Legends of Carrick*, first published in 1854, with stories from Carrick-on-Suir. Every signpost points to a story preserved in a name or events it has been witness to. I have tried here to pick a selection from across the generations and geography of Tipperary.

The majority of this material has come from the treasure trove accessible in the National Folklore Archives in UCD, from the Schools Collection in the 1930s and later collections made by Seosamh O'Dálaigh in the area around Two-Mile-Borris in the 1940s and '50s. I can't say enough about how valuable those collections are, nor how greatly I admire and appreciate the ideals of those responsible, who created and curated such an extensive collection. Materials from the Tipperary Schools Collection will soon be available to view online through www.duchas.ie. Other sources include old manuscripts of the first millennium, translations of which can be viewed online though UCC's Copus of Electronic Texts at www.ucc.ie/celt.

There is another great source of local stories which I haven't tapped on this occasion, and that is the many individuals living across the county who carry on the stories from generations past, adding to the folklore of a new generation. Every community has such men and women, and their position is an important one. I hope though, that this collection might feed a curiosity which will lead to a greater interest in our local stories, not just in Tipperary but right across the country, creating opportunities for those storytellers and lore-keepers to share their stories, wit and in-depth knowledge of their own localities.

About
Tipperary

For those of you not already familiar with Tipperary, let me give you a picture. Tipperary is the second-largest county in Ireland. It is an inland county, surrounded by eight other counties and bordered by two main rivers: to the west, the River Shannon with Lough Derg and counties Galway, Limerick and Clare; to the north, County Offaly; to the east, counties Laois and Kilkenny; and to the south, counties Waterford and Cork with the River Suir. There are other smaller rivers which are tributaries either to the River Shannon or River Suir. The mountain ranges of the county include: the Galtee Mountains, which border counties Clare, Limerick and Cork; the Silvermine Mountains a little further north; the Arra Hills to the west, which lie between Killaloe and Nenagh; the Knockmealdown Mountains, which form part of the southern border with County Waterford; Slievenamon, which lies between Fethard and Carrick-on-Suir; and the Devil's Bit up near the Offaly border. In the centre, lies the Golden Vale, a rich, fertile rolling pasture for which Tipperary is prized.

Tipperary has a rich and coloured history. The Danes were present from the ninth century and the Vikings came in the tenth century, ransacking the monasteries and causing havoc, leading to the emergence of leaders like Brian Boru. The Normans came in the twelfth and thirteenth centuries, building forts and strongholds, and dividing the county into its twelve baronies. Many of them remained, settling to become permanent features of the county's history. Cromwell arrived in the 1640s, leaving his mark across many of the towns, communities and monasteries, both physically and psychologically. His name still sends a shiver through a person's spine, with stories of hunted priests, murder and violence, and even some tales of hidden treasures still waiting to be found.

The famine affected Tipperary badly, and there are both horrific stories highlighting the indifference of absentee landlords (like Lord Portarlington, who came to feast while his people suffered and returned to England leaving only £100 to help the afflicted) and stories of great generosity and hope. The apathy those abusive landlords showed led to the formation of groups like 'the Whiteboys', some of whom could be just as ruthless as the landlords they were standing up to, and later inspired the likes of Thomas McDonnagh, Charles Kickham and Daniel Breen to work both politically and through revolution for better conditions and a free Ireland.

Like any other county, Tipperary also has its sports heroes and heroines, musicians, entrepreneurs, storytellers and advocates. The local websites and parish pages carry lists of the sons and daughters in whom they take pride. It is a county today famed for its historical and ecclesiastical sites and places of natural beauty. A county feared for its hurlers. Above all it is a place well worth visiting, and I hope some of the stories here might entice you to do so. You might even feel inspired to gather the ones I've missed.

Aideen McBride, 2015

1

FROM LONG AGO

So let's start at the beginning. There was once a time when there were no people living on the island of Ireland, before it was ever called Ireland. There was a time before the rivers had sprung or the mountains were raised. In that beginning there came the very first settlers. Like most counties, Tipperary has a history which reaches back into the mythology of Ireland, but unlike most other counties Tipperary can claim a link with the very first settlers to Ireland. Here is that story.

FIONNTAN MAC BOCHAN TOUNTINNA OF THE ARRA HILLS

Back in biblical times, Noah was working on his ark. He gathered the wood and materials to build it and then collected together all the animals as God had told him, at the same time preparing his family for what lay ahead. However, not all of Noah's children were permitted onto the ark; some it seems had chosen lives of theft and lies and there was no place for them in the new world Noah was to build. Noah's son Bith was one of those denied passage on the ark, but Bith's daughter Cessair promised to lead her father and friends to safety if they would follow her. She would take them west, to the edge of the known world, to a land where no people had ever been and no sin had ever been committed and hopefully there they could start a new life and escape the flood.

The group headed off, the journey was treacherous and there were storms and high seas. Cessair, Bith and their companions finally landed on the shores of Corca Duibhne, in County Kerry, shortly before the time of the Great Flood. But it had been a hazardous journey and two of their three boats were lost on the way. The group of travellers who had survived was made up of fifty women, including Cessair, but only three men, Bith, Ladhra and Fionntan mac Bochra. It is they who finally alighted on the shore of Ireland, tired and weary from their long journey.

These were the first people to inhabit Ireland and they brought with them the first sheep to come to this island. They began to build a new life for themselves, but as there were only three men, the women began fighting over which of them would get to be married. The women decided they would have to share husbands. While each man had a principal wife, they also had fifteen other wives. Cessair married Fionntan. It was a tough job caring for all those wives and Fionntan found it particularly difficult but he managed as best he could.

Ladhra died soon after at a place named Ard Ladhrann on the Wexford coast, he was the first person to die in Ireland and is remembered as the first person to be buried on the island. When he died his wives were divided between Bith and Fionntan. Bith died not long after Ladhra and is believed to be buried under the cairn that bears his name on Slieve Beatha in County Fermanagh. Fionntan was left to care for all the women. This was too much for poor Fionntan so he ran away, and hid in a cave in the Arra Hills.

Soon after that the flood came and covered all the land with water. Fionntan, hiding in the cave in the Arra Hills, escaped the worst, but he was the only one high enough to escape the water, he alone survived the flood, Cessair and the other women and their children all dying. The cave in which Fionntan had taken refuge became known as *Tonn Tuinne,* 'the height of the flood'; today it is known as Tountinna and is the highest point on the Arra Hills.

Alone in the land, Fionntan passed his time changing form. Sometimes he was a salmon, swimming through the rivers; sometimes an eagle flying to great heights. He lived to a great age, 5,000 years, and saw the coming of other races to Ireland: the Fir Bolg, the Formorians, the Tuath Dé Dannan and the Milesians. Fionntan noticed and noted all that happened on the island during his long lifetime, and if ever a king needed advice or guidance Fionntan was there to give it, as he did for Diarmuid Mac Cearrbheoil, High King of Ireland, towards the beginning of his reign about the proper manner of procedure according to the ancient way of things; no one could remember but Fionntan, who had witnessed how things had been done long ago, was able to direct Diarmuid. Shortly after his meeting with Diarmuid, Fionntan passes out of Irish history. Some believe he left Ireland to the new beliefs in the safe hands of Christianity.

'If I had lived Fintan's years' is a phrase that can still be heard said.

Bodb Derg

During the time of Fionntan, but before the coming of our race, the Tuath Dé Dannan ruled over Ireland. The Tuath Dé Dannan were a race of gods, with near immortality, who ruled in Ireland after the Fir Bolg. It was they who defeated Balor of the Evil Eye and the Formorians who had come from the sea. They brought music and feasting, war and healing. And in the time when they held most power – before their defeat at the battle of Tailtin after which they removed themselves to homes beneath the earth, emerging only from time to time – they had their own places of importance and ritual in Ireland. Among those were the raths, dwelling places of theirs which were dotted across the county. One of these was Sidh-ar-Feman on Slievenamon, the home of Bodb Derg.

There are a number of stories which involve Bodb Derg, the grandfather of the Children of Lir. Bodb had fostered the three daughters of Oilell of Aran and two of these had married King Lir, the second turning her niece and three nephews into swans out of jealousy, in what is probably one of the most well-known stories of Irish mythology. But there are other stories involving Bodb and here are two of them, one with that familiar theme of turning into swans. Both are stories of love and longing.

CROTTA CLIACH – THE HARPS OF CLIACH

Cliach was a harper to Smirdubh MacSmal, king of the three Rosses in Connacht, and he was a good harper. He had fallen hopelessly in love with the daughter of Bodb Derg, but she had no interest in him. He came to Slievenamon where Sidh-ar-Femhin stood, and began to play his harp. He played his harp beautifully and sang sweetly, but to no avail. Bodb's daughter was not interested, and Bodb was not impressed. He drew up a mist over the rath so that Cliach could not see it, and would not be able to enter. Cliach did not give up. He moved back a bit to the hills of the Galtee Mountains, nearly 30 miles away, and continued to play and sing. Sometimes he played two harps at the same time to show his skill, playing the most beautiful music, but still the daughter of Bodh showed no interest. She did not even acknowledge the beautiful music and she never came to him. He played for the whole of another year, but to no avail. Her heart was not softened; she had no love for Cliach.

Cliach was heartbroken. The earth on which he stood was not as hardened as Bodb's daughter's heart and it opened and cracked. A lake formed on the hill and from it came a dragon which took Cliach and dragged him down into its depths. The lake became known as The Mouth of the Dragon or in Irish *Loch Béal Dragan*, today known as Lough Muskry. Those hills were known as *Crotta Cliach* – 'the Harps of Cliach'. Today we know them better as the Galtee Mountains, and sometimes on a quiet day, when the wind is soft, you can still hear echoes of Cliach playing on the wind.

There is a lovely walk through the Galtee's up to Lough Muskry. The name Muskery comes from Cairbe Musc, son of Con of the Hundred Battles, who lived in that area at one time. Some come to see if they can hear the music of Cliach still in the air, some to see if there is any sign of the three times fifty beautiful maidens (who you'll hear about in the next story), some just to admire the scene and find the lake hidden among the hills ready to surprise the unwary traveller. If you like walking and haven't been there yet, then go.

If the lake was brought into being through a story of unrequited love, there is another story of the lake which has a happier ending.

AONGHUS' LOVE SICKNESS

Aonghus was the half-brother to Bodb Derg by his father the Dagda. His mother was Boinn, who gave her name to the river Boyne. Aonghus lived at Brugh na Bóinne with his mother.

One night he had a dream, an *aisling* or vision. He saw a beautiful woman approach him, but just as he reached out to touch her she disappeared. The following night he had the same dream with the same result, just as he reached out to touch her she disappeared. Every night for a year he had this dream and he was growing sick with longing and love. A doctor was sent for and, after examining Aonghus, he called for Boinn.

'Boinn,' he said, 'Your son suffers from a love sickness and unless the maiden be found of whom he dreams he is lost.'

Boinn lost no time and went at once to search all of Ireland for the maiden Aonghus described from his dream. At the end of a year she had had no luck. Boinn called for Dagda, Aonghus' father.

'Dagda,' she said, 'Aonghus suffers from a love sickness and unless the maiden be found he is lost.'

Dagda lost no time, he went to his son Bodb Derg at Sidh-ar-Femin on Slievenamon. He explained the story to Bodb and described the maiden Aonghus had seen in his dream. Hearing the description of the visionary woman, Bodb recognised her as a form who had been seen on *Loch Béal Dragan*. Bodb told Dagda to take Aonghus to *Loch Béal Dragan* (Lough Muskry) at Samhain (the night joining the last day of October and the first day of November), and that there he would see the vision of his dream.

The Dagda took Aonghus to *Loch Béal Dragan* at Samhain. There Aonghus saw three times fifty beautiful maidens with silver chains about them, and the one with a golden chain. She was the vision from his dream. But how to meet her? Who was she?

Aonghus was anxious to learn who this maiden was, that he might talk with her. When they returned to Bodb he was able to tell them that she was Caer, the daughter of Eathal Anbhuail of Sidh Uamhain in Connacht, and that she was not of this world but of the otherworld. Dagda went to Queen Maebh, the Queen of Connacht, told her the tale and asked if she could help them meet Caer. Maebh sent for Ethal Anbhuail; he arrived but explained that he had no power to grant his daughter to Aonghus as wife. She was under an enchantment, one year in one form, one year in another. If Aonghus had seen her that Samhain as a young maiden then the following Samhain she would be in the form of a swan.

The next year Aonghus returned to *Loch Béal Dragan* at Samhain. There on the lake were three times fifty swans with silver chains about them and among them one with a golden chain. Aonghus went to the water and called to Caer. She turned and came toward him, as she neared he too was turned into a swan. They flew three times around the lake and then left for Brugh na Bóinne.

There, their sweet singing sent everyone asleep. Aonghus and Caer remained there at Brugh na Bóinne, together.

SENCHÁN TORPEIST

Senchán was one of the great Irish poets from the seventh century. His father was from the Arra sept of the North Tipperary–Limerick border area, an area which Senchán's surviving work shows he was familiar with.

Senchán was a much-travelled man; he was at the convention of poets in Derry in AD 575, and a favourite of King Guaire in Connacht. He was appointed chief *ollamh* – chief poet of Ireland – but my favourite story is of his visit to the Isle of Man. It wasn't unusual for poets or poetesses to go travelling at this time; likely it was a way to gain inspiration and find muses. There had once been a famous poetess in East Limerick by the name of Ingen of the Uí Fidhgheinte clan who had gone on a circuit of Ireland, Scotland and the Isle of Man but who had never returned. No one knew what had happened to her.

Senchán though, wasn't planning on going missing, he took a great retinue of poets with him, fifty in all, and they all set off. Just as their boat was pulling off however a man called to them from the shore to bring him with them. Senchán turned back and there on the shore was the ugliest man he had ever seen. The man had a great lump protruding from his forehead which was oozing puss, his clothes were filthy and torn and he was crawling with lice.

'Bring me with you,' called the man, 'I'll be better company for you than those haughty men who think they are poets.' Senchán, amused by the man's wit, decided to bring him along. When they reached the Isle of Man they met a tall old woman on the shore, gathering winkles. Senchán told her who they were and where they were from. She challenged them in poetry, and her words were so well formed that Senchán and his companions were hard pressed to come up with suitable replies and they soon gave up. But the stranger, the ugly old man crawling with lice and oozing puss, answered her, and spoke in such a poetical manner that he was declared winner of the contest. During the course of the dialogue between the old woman and ugly man, Senchán realised that the old woman was none other than the famous Ingen, the missing poetess of East Limerick and he invited her to return to Ireland in the boat with them. As they travelled back Senchán noticed that the old ugly man was changing. He was no longer crawling with lice, nor was the puss oozing from his head – in fact, the lump on his forehead seemed to be reducing in size. By the time the coast of Ireland had come into view he had transformed into a handsome young man. As soon as they reached the shore he disappeared, for he was the Spirit of Poetry who had accompanied them on their journey.

Senchán is probably best remembered as the one who found the lost story of *Táin Bó Cúailnge* – The Cattle Raid of Cooley. Now maybe you are one of the many who have heard the great epic tale, which tells how Queen Maebh, growing jealous of her husband's acquired goods, sent her soldiers to take the great bull of Cooley for her own. This led to a great battle between the men of Connacht under Maebh and the men of Ulster. But the men of Ulster, finding themselves afflicted with a sickness at that time, had none to defend them but Cúchulainn himself. The great poem tells the story of the battle, the lead up to the battle and the fallout afterwards. However, were it not for Senchán you would never have heard the story at all, for it was lost to the people of Ireland. A great sage had taken the manuscript to the east, leaving another manuscript in return, and other than snippets of the poem remembered by poets here and there in the country, the greater part of the story had been lost and forgotten.

One time, while a guest of King Guaire, Senchán tried the patience and generosity of the king. At that time poets had great power. Anyone who did not make them welcome or answer their requests, or give them what they wanted, could find themselves the subject of one of their satires and these satires were not only damaging to a person's reputation, but were also, in some cases, believed to have a cursing effect; whatever ill a poet might wish upon a king or chieftain was sure to come to pass. For example, at one time it was said that Senchán, upset by the actions of rats who had gnawed or nibbled into his food, composed a satire of four lines which resulted in ten of the said rats falling dead immediately.

On this occasion Guaire's patience and generosity were spent and exhausted. He was sick of Senchán and his demands, so he asked Senchán to recite a poem for him.

'Of course your majesty,' said Senchán, 'What poem will I recite for you?'

'*Táin Bó Cúailnge*!' demanded Guaire.

But Senchán couldn't; he didn't know the poem and he was insulted. Guaire well knew the poem was not to be had but Senchán had no choice but to search for any remains of the lost poem. He visited many poets, some of whom remembered bits and pieces of the lost work, but still there were huge tracts missing. Then Senchán met with his half-brother, St Cillian of Fenagh, in County Leitirm. Senchán and Cillian had the same mother, but

Cillian's father was a direct descendant of King Fergus mac Róich. Fergus Mac Roích had been alive during the Cattle Raid of Cooley and part of the events of that time.

In fact, he had been king until his nephew Conor Mac Nessa tricked him out of it. When Naoise had run away with Conor's intended bride Deirdre, Conor sent Fergus to tell them it was ok to return home; but when they did Conor killed them all. That was the last straw for Fergus and he defected from Conor and Ulster into the service of Queen Maebh in Connacht, the same Queen Maebh who sent the men to take the brown bull of Cooley.

Together, Senchán, Cillian and some saintly friends of Cillian including Colmcille, Ciaran of Clonmacnoise and Brendan of Birr went to the grave side of Fergus. They kept vigil there, fasting for three days and nights. On the third day Fergus appeared to them, sat with them and recited the story of Táin Bó Cúailnge in its entirety, and St Cillian wrote down all that Fergus said. Ciaran of Clonmacnoise gave the cow (his favourite) to provide the hide to make the velum onto which the poem was written and it is one of the passages included in the Book of Dun Cow, preserved today in the library of the Royal Irish Academy.

The next time you hear mention of the story of *Táin Bó Cúailnge*, remember just how close we were to never having a chance to hear it at all, and it being lost forever.

Sources

Fionntan Mac Bochan/Toutinne of the Arra Hills: *Annals of the Four Masters, Myths Legends and Romance*

Crotta Cliach – The Harps of Cliach and Aonghus' Love Sickness: *The Book of the Galtees and Golden Vein*; local web-sites; *'Myth Legends and Romance' The Prose Tales in the Rennes Dindshenchas*; *The Book of The Galtees and Golden Vein by Paul J. Flynn* (Hodges, Figgs and Co., 1926)

Senchán Torpeist: *Source Book of Leinster*

2

AN GOBÁN
SAOR

In ancient times in Ireland there were many craftsmen of wood, metal and stone. Some were greater than others and were master craftsmen, and some were so skilled they were sought out not only in their own districts and counties, but from other countries and further afield as well.

The Gobán Saor was one of those highly skilled master craftsmen (Gobán is from the Irish word for 'smith' or 'craftsman' and an Gobán Saor was one of the best). He is said to have had a hand in some of the oldest and most impressive buildings in Ireland, including St Moling's church and Ferns Castle. Mind you, there is probably many a building where people would like everyone to think that they were wealthy enough or sensible enough to have employed the Gobán Soar, and maybe he had no hand there at all.

The Gobán Soar, by all accounts, was not only a master craftsman but a sensible man too. He and his wife had been married a long time when she died, leaving the craftsman and his grown son Darra to fend for themselves. Now the Gobán Saor had no aversion to hard work, building and hauling, chiselling and hammering but cooking and cleaning did not come under his remit and it wasn't long till they felt the want of a good woman about their place.

One day the Gobán Saor called his son to him. 'Son,' said he, 'I could never replace your mother but if you were to find a good, hard-working woman for a wife, we could have our cooking and cleaning looked after.' And he sent his son on an errand to find a good and clever wife for himself. Darra was to travel to the market with a sheep skin for sale. It was a beautiful soft skin with the wool still on it and Darra was to return with the skin and the price of it.

Darra thought this an impossible task, for who would buy the skin and then give it away again? But he did as his father asked and went to the fair. All day long many young women admired the sheep skin and asked the price of it, when they heard that the young man meant to be paid the price of the skin and yet take the skin away with him they soon walked away.

That evening Darra was returning home with the sheep skin and he fell into walking beside a young woman on the road. She too admired his sheep skin and asked him how much he wanted.

'The price of the skin and the skin,' he said expecting that she too would walk away. She handled the skin for a while, 'Yes,' she said, 'I think we can agree on that, come to my father's house and we'll settle the bargain.' And she brought the surprised son of the Gobán Saor to her father's house.

When they got there she got a pair of shears and began to shear the wool from the sheep skin, she weighed the wool gave the son the price of it and returned the shorn skin to him. Delighted he went his way and returned to tell the story to his father. When his father saw the skin and heard the story he was delighted and encouraged Darra to pursue the young woman. Well, soon the two were married and the son and his wife and the Gobán Saor lived quite happily together.

꧁

The Gobán Saor and Darra worked together for many years, and there is one particular happening during their years of work which is widely told of, though the precise location is not agreed on. Some say it was in Munster or Connacht, England or Wales. In all versions, however, the particulars are pretty much the same. I've taken the first version of the story I came across and set it in Wales.

The Gobán went from strength to strength, all the time improving upon what he had already done or learned. He was kept very busy as messengers came from all across Ireland to ask him to work for some king or abbot or other. Whatever the Gobán Saor built today was sure to be the best and finest that had ever been built but whatever he built tomorrow was sure to be even better again.

One time the king of Wales sent word that he wished the Gobán Saor to come and build for him the finest castle that had ever been. Off he and his son went to build the castle; after all, it was not every day a king of Wales sent for you. They worked away on the castle, and the king was duly impressed. But it was the king's intention to kill the Gobán Soar when he was finished his work so that he could never build a castle better than his. The Gobán Saor became wise to the fact that he and his son were in danger.

One day he came to the king and said, 'Your majesty, your castle is almost finished.' The king was delighted, 'But,' continued the Gobán Saor, 'to put the final finishing touches on it I need a tool which I have left in Ireland. I'll have to return home and get it.'

'Oh no, no, no,' said the King, 'I can't allow that. What if you didn't return, then the castle would never be finished. I'm sure we have the tool here in my kingdom. I'll have it fetched.'

'I doubt that,' said the Gobán Saor, 'It is a tool of my own invention which is the mark of my work. There is only the one of it and that is at home in Rathgobbin.'

'Then we'll send someone to fetch it,' said the king.

'But my daughter-in-law would not give it to just anyone,' said the Gobán Saor, 'It would have to be myself or my son or someone of royal blood.'

'Then I'll send my son to fetch it,' said the king of Wales.

The Gobán Saor wrote out a note with the name of the tool on it for the young prince to take with him and he was sent off to Rathgobbin to fetch this tool. Now no such tool existed and what the Gobán Saor had written on the note was *'Cor in aghaidh an caim'*, meaning 'crooked against crooked'.

The prince got to Ireland and came to Rathgobbin where the Gobán Saor's daughter-in-law was waiting for the return of her husband and father-in-law. When she read the note the Gobán Saor sent she knew something was wrong. She brought the prince to a room and told him that the tool he was sent for was at the back of the room on a high shelf. Once the prince stepped into the room she locked the door, trapping him inside, then she sent a message back to the king of Wales.

'I will release your son to you once my husband and the Gobán Saor are returned safe to me.' The king, knowing he was beaten, released the master craftsman and his son without delay and they returned to Ireland. The prince was released and returned to Wales. Which of the great castles of Wales was the one he built I'm not sure but it's probably one of the ones still standing.

An Gobán Saor and Holy Cross Abbey

The story is also told that at the building of Holy Cross Abbey near Thurles in County Tipperary, a middle-aged man with greying hair arrived one day, poorly dressed with his bag of tools over his shoulder. He was tired and foot sore and obviously had been travelling a great distance. He asked to see the foreman.

'God Bless the work,' he said.

'God bless the spokesman,' answered the foreman.

'I'm looking for work,' said the stranger, 'I've been travelling from place to place, could you help me on my way?'

The foreman looked him up and down, not thinking much of him, 'What are you good for?' he asked.

'Ah, not much,' answered the stranger.

'You look it,' replied the foreman with contempt. 'But we'll give you a trial, there's a piece of stone for you. We're just going to dinner, see can you cut me out a cat with two tails,' and, saying that, he gave the call for lunch and left the man to his work.

As soon as their backs were turned, the stranger opened up his bag, took out his mallet and chisel and set to work. Before the diners were finished he had carved out a cat with two tails that was so real looking you would think it was going to pounce. He tidied up his tools, put them back in his bag, the bag over his shoulder and off he headed towards Cashel on his journey again.

He had hardly put his foot to the road when the foreman and his workers returned from their dinners and saw the beautifully carved cat with two tails. They stopped in surprise and all admired the fine work.

'Who is he,' they asked one another, 'that can carve so finely?' An old, grey-haired mason came forward and examined the work, 'That,' he said, 'Was the Gobán Saor himself. There isn't a man living could do work like that but himself.'

'Lads,' said the foreman, 'I'm ashamed of myself. Divide yourselves into groups and go after him, he can't be gone far, and bring him back here by whatever means.' The workmen divided into groups and headed out in all directions as fast as they could to catch up with the master craftsman and bring him back, but search as they did, far and near, they couldn't find him.

There was nothing they could do, but they installed the carving of the cat with two tails into the building of Holy Cross Abbey.

There are many other stories relating to An Gobán Saor, his work and adventures of which most counties can boast a part, but his story ends in Tipperary. An Gobán Saor is buried in Derrynaflan in the heart of the Bog of Allen, not far from the church on the ancient monastic site. If you go there today you can still see the three grave markers, one for the grave of the Gobán Saor and, they say, the other two for his wife and son.

Sources
Myths Legends and Romance by Dáithí Ó hÓgáin; *My Clonmel Scrapbook*

3

SLIEVENAMON

Slievenamon is a mountain which stands noticeably on the land-scape of Tipperary between Clonmel, Fethard and the Kilkenny boarder. The name *Sliabh na mBan* means 'the mountain of the women'.

There are different accounts of how the mountain got its name, all concerning Fionn MacCumhail and a race. This is one of my favourites.

Fionn MacCumhail was a great hero of Ireland. In his youth, all the young women were chasing after him, and Fionn had his pick of them. There were many he loved, but three in particular he had loved in such a way as to make a father of him. Now the rules of the time were such that a man could have no more than one wife at any one time. Fionn had promised each of these three women that he would marry them, and now they were calling on him to honour his promise. Fionn was in a pickle, he genuinely did love all three and he couldn't decide which to pick to marry. He couldn't be seen to keep a promise to one and not the other. Maybe he felt a little like Fionntan with the 150 wives, for he took a page from that book and ran away.

He ran up to the top of the mountain on the plain of Femen and hid. But the three women were resourceful, and were bonded to each other by their common complaint. They tracked Fionn and found him on the top of the mountain.

'Fionn,' they cried, 'You promised you'd marry me.'

'You promised you'd marry me.'

'You promised you'd marry me.'

Fionn was faced by the three women and tried to comfort them and cajole them, talking about how he wished he could marry all three of them but that wasn't allowed and what was he to do, while all the time giving a sly wink to first one and then another, as if to say, 'But it's really you I want to marry.'

This did not have the desired effect and the three women demanded that he choose one of them to marry.

'Ok,' said Fionn, 'Give me three days to work out a plan as to how to choose between you.' The women agreed to that and went away to return in the three days, each sure that it would be they and not one of the others who would marry Fionn. Now Fionn felt miserable, the kind of miserable that can be eased by landing into the first *bothán* or meeting house he could find and drowning his sorrows in *poitín* or whiskey and company. But he didn't do that. He held out against the temptation and instead cut himself a stick to use as a pole vault to take him from hill to hill, over rivers and streams and across plains, until he got to a wise friend in the north who might be able to help him in his predicament.

Three days later Fionn was back and seated cross-legged at the foot of the mountain. He was dressed not in the fine clothes he usually wore but in his hunting gear of animal skins. The three women arrived and saw him sitting there and to them he looked even more handsome than ever.

'Well,' they asked, 'Have you decided which of us you are going to marry?'

'Ladies,' said Fionn, 'How could I ever chose between you? I love each of you equally and would marry all three of you if I could. I can make no choice between you; you are each equally beautiful, each equally clever and each equally industrious, so I have come up with a plan. I will sit and wait at the top of this mountain here and the three of you will set off from the same point at the same

time. The first one to reach me I will marry there and then. And,'
he continued, seeing the three look at one another and scrunch
their faces, 'if it should be that natural causes cut that union short
I will marry the others of you in turn.'

The three women weren't altogether happy but they could see
that the race was probably the fairest way of choosing, so they
agreed. Up to the top of the mountain went Fionn, and the
three women took their place at the starting line. At the arranged
moment they set off. Fionn watched from the top of the mountain. Now if Fionn said that he didn't care which of the three won
he was lying, because he had one woman who he sincerely hoped
wouldn't win and that was the red-haired woman. Fionn watched
as the women raced, first one in the lead then another, then one
stumbled but got back up again, then another gained and passed
the first out. The three women raced on up the mountain each
eager to be the winner. Fionn watched in horror as the red-headed
woman caught up in the last few paces and passed the other two
women to win the race. He was not pleased but he had made
his promise that the first woman to reach him he would marry
then and there, and he had to keep his word. He married the red-
headed woman but cursed the mountain.

'Mountain of Women should be barren as it gave the red-headed
woman to Fionn.'

After the race it is said that Fionn, returning from the mountain,
stopped to rest at Slieveardagh by River Guineagh (*Abhainn an
Ri* – the king's river) where he feasted on salmon and berries.

Sources
Handerhan the Fairyman & Legends of Carrick by John O'Neil
(1854)

4

CASHEL AND ITS KINGS

The Rock of Cashel is quite a landmark; the first time you see the rock upon the horizon is a moment you won't easily forget. There are many stories concerning the rock over the years, from its relationship to the 'Devil's Bit' from whence it was bitten and then spat, to the people who lived on or near the rock and the strange things which happened to them.

THE FINDING OF CASHEL

Just before St Patrick arrived as bishop in Ireland, two swine herds, Duirdriu and Cuiririan, were herding their pigs in County Tipperary, near where the great Rock of Cashel stands. Every year they would come to spend about three months on the site with their pigs.

One night, the two swineherds stayed at Clais Duirdrenn to the north of the rock. That night they shared a vision where they witnessed St Patrick's arrival to Ireland. The following night they had a second vision: a magnificent feast was laid before them and, while they ate, an angel announced that the first person to light a fire on Cashel would become King of Munster.

Each of the swine herds returned to their own people and their own kings, for they were from different clans; Duirdriu to Conall

Mac Nenta Con, King of Ely, and Cuiririan to Luightheach, King of Muscraige. Luightheach's son, Conall Corc, was present as Cuiririan told of the vision and straight away he set out for the rock to light the fire there. He also prepared a great feast and sent Cuiririan with invitations to all the local chieftains and kings to attend. Meanwhile, Duirdriu told his king the story and Conall Mac Nenta Con consulted his druids who told him the prophecy was a true one. As much as this displeased him, Cashel was on his land so he headed off to the feast. Conall Corc made him very welcome. So much so that Conall Mac Nenta Coc requested Duirdriu to give Conall Corc a blessing proclaiming him King of Munster.

Duirdriu did so and from that day on the Uí Druidrenn, the descendants of Duirdriu, were given the role of proclaiming every King of Munster. This blessing from the Uí Druidrenn would protect the kings from violent death unless they neglected to uphold truth and justice. Thus Cashel came to be the seat of the Kings of Munster, a place as important to events in Munster as the Hill of Tara is to Ireland and Armagh to Ulster.

CONALL CORC, FIRST KING OF CASHEL

Who was this Conall mac Luightheach who became the first king of Cashel, the first of the Eoganachta line? He was born around AD 340, the son of Luightheach, King of the Muscairge, and grandson of Eoghan Mór from whom the Eoganacht take their name, nephew to Crimthann Mór Mac Fidaig, King of Munster and High King of Ireland.

His mother was a woman known as Boilce ban Breathanach, a satirist and poet of the Britons and the story is that she put Luightheach 'faoi ghease', under an unbreakable promise, to sleep with her and so Conall was conceived. On the night Conall was born, Boilce was in the palace of Luightheach and also present was Feidhilm, the daughter of a witch. Boilce put Conall into the foster care of Feidhilm.

Feidhilm took Conall to live with her, but when there were other witches around she would hide Conall beneath the stone of the hearth to keep him safe. One day a witch came saying, 'I will destroy nothing except that which lies beneath the hearth' and she sent a bolt of fire across the hearth which burned the ear of Conall, leaving a redish-purple mark that earned him his nickname, 'corc', which means 'purple'.

Another time a learned man examined the hands of Conall. 'You,' he said, 'are to set free captives and hostages wherever you go as in doing so you will be famous.'

At that time Crimthanm Mór Mac Fidaig was High King of Ireland. He had no heirs, but Conall was a fosterling to him as both their fathers were brothers. Crimthan, as High King of Ireland, was entitled to a tribute of sixty cows from the people of Leinster and he sent Conall to collect this tribute. When Conall arrived to collect the tribute he found a great argument taking place as to a captive there called Gruibne. With the cows Conall had collected for his uncle, he ransomed Gruibne who then went free to Scotland. In another place in Leinster, Conall ransomed another two captives; one of these he took with him and the other he was to return for, but before he returned that man was killed by nineteen of his relations. They gave Conall a score of cows and a score of bridles each, as blood fine for the murder.

Conall returned to Crimthann with 380 cows and the 380 bridles. He gave Crimthann the sixty cows he had been sent to collect along with sixty bridles. The rest of cows and bridles Conall then divided among the warriors of Ormond, earning for himself a great name. Crimthann became jealous of Conall's success and, encouraged by his wife, plotted to be rid of him. He sent Conall to Scotland to Feradach, King of the Picts. On Conall's shield Crimthann had a message inscribed in ogham writing, telling Feradach to kill Conall. Conall was not able to read the ogham script so was unaware of the message he was carrying.

When he arrived in Scotland there was a great snow storm and Conall became trapped in a snow drift. Cold and exposed, he was

near dead when Gruibne, now a local swineherd, found him and pulled him out. Gruibne was able to read the ogham script and saw the message on Conall's shield. He told Conall what Crimthan had written and then changed the message so it read in Conall's favour. When Conall met with Feradach he was greeted warmly. He settled in well and had soon married the daughter of the King of the Picts. For seven years Conall remained in Scotland and had three sons with his wife but there was part of him which longed for home. When at last Crimthann died he felt he could once again return to Ireland. He did and made his way to Munster.

Not long after this the two swineherds had their vision and Conall lit the fire to become King of Munster. The rest of his kingship seems to have passed quietly enough, and the kings of Munster were direct descendants of Conall up to AD 960, when Mahon Mac Cinnéide of the Dal Cais Sept became King of Munster. He was brother to maybe the most famous king of them all – Brian Boru.

BAPTISM OF AENGUS MAC NATHFRACH

Conall Corc's grandson, Aengus Mac Nathfrach, became King of Munster around AD 453. He was the first king of Munster to be baptised, not that that was an easy job. Aengus liked to be sure before he went and made a big decision, and becoming a Christian meant leaving many of the old customs and rituals behind. St Declan had been working on converting him for years, but Aengus was having none of it, even with his sons becoming Christians he still hadn't made up his mind. The idea was sinking in though and slowly and surely he was convinced and converted. It was St Patrick who had the honour of baptising Aengus at the Rock of Cashel.

Now, Aengus was a grown man when he was baptised and he had not been to too many baptisms before his own, so he wasn't too familiar with the format of the ceremony. There was a great crowd gathered to witness this event; a king becoming a Christian, leaving the old ways, disbanding the druids and dispensing with magic in favour of this new teaching about Jesus was a big deal. During the ceremony St Patrick's crozier pressed onto Aengus' foot. It pressed so hard into his foot it pierced it till it bled but Aengus thought this was a part of the ceremony and so he still did not cry out. It wasn't until after it was all over he learned that there was no foot piercing involved in baptism.

That same crozier – *Bachal Iosa*, 'staff of Jesus' – was kept in Armagh up to 1178, when it was brought to Christ Church in Dublin. You might have been able to see it today only it was destroyed during the reformation in 1528.

It was common in those days for a king to keep hostages; the king would make an agreement with another king, leave his hostages with the other and take hostages of the other with him. This way each were sure to keep their side of the agreement and if they didn't the other side had the right to kill their hostages. It was a matter of honour that each king would take very good care of the hostages in their keeping; if anything should happen to them it could mean war with the other side.

Now Aengus had seven hostages in his keeping, and he looked after them well, but one time a plague hit Cashel and the seven hostages died all on the same night. Aengus was in a state. He kept the news of their deaths from their families but he knew he couldn't lie to them for much longer and it would bring shame to his reign that such a thing would happen to men in his care and under his protection.

St Declan happened to call the following day, and Aengus was pleased to see him.

'Oh Declan,' he said, 'You who serve the one true God, help me in my need and bring back to life those seven hostages who were put in my charge, for I am ashamed of their deaths and fear their people will blame me and make war on us.'

'Only the only Son of God, Jesus, can bring the dead back to life,' said St Declan, 'but I will see what I can do.'

St Declan was brought to the place where the seven corpses lay, they were all young men and had been in the prime of their lives. Declan sprinkled them with holy water and prayed. The corpses began to move and their eyelids opened.

'Rise up and give praise to God,' said Declan and the seven men rose and praised God. St Declan left then, but all remembered, who had seen the miracle.

BRIAN BORU AND THE BATTLE OF SOLOHEAD

Brian Boru was the youngest son of Cennide, who was chieftain of the Dal gCais. He was born in AD 926 and lived in County Clare, just across the River Shannon from Tipperary. When he was about twelve years old a Viking raid came to his village and his father was killed. His oldest brother Lahtna took over chieftainship of the Dal gCais, followed by his brother Mahon, who went on to become the first King of Munster from outside the Eoghnacht clan. The Vikings had a very strong base in Limerick and there are many stories of their raiding parties coming to the towns and villages on the western side of Tipperary. Mahon attempted to make peace with the Vikings and an alliance was formed with the 'foreigner' king, King Ivar in Limerick. Ivar was known as a tyrant, though and his ships had arrived in a fleet greater than the locals had ever known. He had appointed chiefs and kings to the localities, and bailiffs to collect the tax, and positioned a soldier in every household. Such an air of fear lay across the country at that time that an Irishman could show no devotion to his priest or chief, to the sick or dying for fear of the Danes. What little food a family might have, the soldier had to be fed first before anyone else, and if a man could not pay his tax he would have to sell himself into slavery and have his nose cut off.

Mahon thought the best way to deal with such an enemy at that time was to make his alliance with Ivar and hope for peace. But Brian did not agree and he and a group of like-minded men created a band which harassed and harried the Danes and Vikings as much as they could. They were reasonably successful and definitely a thorn in the side of Ivar, but their four-year campaign took its toll and by 968 he had only fifteen followers left. Mahon decided at this stage that peace was not the way to go with Ivar and he joined with his brother Brian in a fight against the Vikings. There were other local leaders too, who on other occasions were not terribly friendly with the Dal gCais but who joined in this fight against a greater enemy.

One day in AD 968 Mahon, Brian and their army left Cashel, and Ivar and his army of over 1,000 men left Limerick. The Irish side sent a small band ahead to be seen by Ivar and lead his army into a wood at Solohead in County Tipperary, just north of Tipperary Town and not far from the Limerick border. The trick worked and the Viking army followed deeper and deeper into the woods before the main Irish army caught them by surprise. The wooded area suited the guerrilla tactics of the Irish. The Vikings, though greater in numbers, were at a disadvantage and couldn't form their wall of shields. The fighting was a bloody battle that lasted from dawn to midday. The Vikings were routed and fled. They were followed by Brian and Mahon who beheaded any they caught on the road. They followed them right back to Limerick city and sacked the city, killing any Vikings they found within.

This was a great victory for the Irish. It stopped the expansion of the Vikings into Ireland, and was the first of three battles Brian Boru fought against the Vikings, the final and most famous being the Battle of Clontarf in 1014. There are many stories about Brian Boru and his deeds in *Clare Folk Tales*.

The Rock of Cashel remained the seat of the Kings of Munster until Brian Boru's grandson Muircheartigh became High King of Ireland in 1101, and gave it to the Church. Work began on the round tower shortly after, and the synod of Cashel took place there in 1172.

Solohead was also the site of another battle, an ambush in 1919 involving Dan Breen of Donohill which sparked off the War of Independence.

There is a romantic mysteriousness which lies about the Rock of Cashel, and it will be no surprise that down the generations there have been many other stories of strange and mysterious happenings associated with the rock. Here are just a few samples from the National Folklore Collection.

Mullins' Shop

Once there was merchant named John Mullins who lived in Cashel. In an effort to help the poor, he got them to work on the Rock of Cashel and paid them for it. One day around dinner time when his two assistants were gone for dinner and he was alone in his shop two friars entered. One spoke: 'Mullins, Stop working on the Rock!'

Mullins answered, 'It's only temporary to help the poor.'

Again the friar repeated, 'Mullins stop working on the rock!'

Then the two friars left.

Mullins went to the door to follow the two friars to argue his case but when he opened the door he couldn't see sight nor sound of them; they had disappeared. Mullins went to the rock that instant and ordered the men to stop working. He never saw the two friars again.

Cashel Cobbler

A cobbler lived in Cashel near the butt of the rock itself. He was always working, mending shoes and making shoes. One evening, a man nearly 7ft high and dressed in poor clothes came in. The cobbler looked up from his work in surprise and a little frightened by the size of the man.

'Good night,' said the stranger.

'Good night,' answered the cobbler.

'Will you make me a pair of shoes?' asked the stranger.

'I will,' answered the cobbler.

'When will they be ready?' asked the stranger.

'This time next week,' answered the cobbler.

'I'll come for them then and it'll be bad for you if they're not ready.'

Then the stranger walked out.

Over the next few days the cobbler bought the bits and bobs he needed to make the stranger's shoes and all was ready the following week when the tall stranger returned to the shop.

'Have you the shoes made?' he asked

'I have,' answered the cobbler, and he got them.

The stranger put them on and then he walked out of the shop. The cobbler still with hammer in hand chased after the stranger, calling after him,

'Hey, you have to pay me for them shoes!'

He followed the man to the graveyard on the Rock of Cashel. Into the graveyard went the stranger and into a vault there at 'The Rock'. As he caught up with the stranger the cobbler raised his hand to hit him with the hammer, but the stranger turned and hit the cobbler in the face, knocking him down.

'You take that, you mane (mean) man. Only for you being so mane (mean) you'd have had the contract for the whole graveyard.' The stranger left then, leaving the cobbler there, on the ground where he was.

Sources

The Finding of Cashel: Senchas Fagbála Caisil; Lobar na Cert CELT UCC

Conall Corc, First King of Cashel: The genealogy of Corca Laidhe UCC CELT; *Myth, Legend and Romance* by Daithi O'Hogán; Conall Corc and the Corco Luigde – Vernam Hull – PMLA Vol.62, no.4 (Dec 1947) pp.892–899 published by Modern Language Association

Baptism of Aengus Mac Nathfrach: Life of St Declan

Brian Boru and the Battle of Solohead: web sources

Mullins' Shop: NFC 700, pp.37–38 collected by Seosamh O'Dálaigh from Joe Fannin, age 79, Two-Mile-Borris, 1940

Cashel Cobbler: NFC 700, p.110 collected by Seosamh O'Dálaigh from Old Foley, age 70, Two-Mile-Borris, 1940

5

SAINTS OF TIPPERARY

It seems there was once a time in Ireland when you couldn't swing a cat without hitting one saint or another. Not only did we have them living in almost every parish, travelling to and fro between each other, bringing great influence and example in our own country, but they travelled Europe too, influencing, teaching and inspiring. Tipperary has its own sons and daughters to add to the lists of people of spiritual influence from the time when we earned the title 'saints and scholars'. There were the daughters of Cainnach who, having been saved from their burning house by St Declan, gave their lives over to prayer; St Columb of Terryglass, who administered the last rites to St Finnian, the teacher of the saints; and St Cera of Kilkrea who founded a convent there. St Patrick too, spent a little time in Tipperary and there are some stories associated with him. These are a sample of some of those who have left their mark in story and place names over the centuries.

ST CATHALDUS OF TARANTO, ITALY (637–685): FEAST DAY 8–10 MAY

St Cathaldus was born Cathal in Canty in County Waterford around 637 and there is a plaque in Balinameela church commemorating the saint. His parents were well off and as a young man they sent him to the school in Lismore, which was the great centre for Christian learning in the South East and attracted students from not only Ireland but from England and Wales as well. Cathal enjoyed study and he soon rose from scholar to teacher. He was noted for his piety and for the miracles which happened through him. He was admired by many but not all; the son of a local chieftain grew jealous of his popularity and reported him to the King of Munster as a magician who was plotting to take over the kingdom. The king gathered an army and headed to Lismore where Cathal was captured and imprisoned in a dungeon until he could be exiled.

Soon, however, the king learned of the mistake, and when the young chieftain died Cathal was offered the lands belonging to that chieftain – the lands of Rachau, now better known as Shanrahan in Clogheen, County Tipperary. Cathal declined – he was a man of God and had no interest in ruling a kingdom – so he was made bishop of the area instead with responsibility over the spiritual wellbeing of the people.

Around the year 667 he set out on pilgrimage to the Holy Land. He went alone and visited many of the holy places there; some say he would have liked to have lived out his life there but it was not to be. On his return voyage his ship was wrecked off the heel of the boot of Italy, near the town of Taranto. Cathal made it to a cave on the coast where he gathered his strength before making his way to the town itself. The town was not a Christian town, if the message of Christianity had been brought there before, it had been long forgotten and the people themselves say that at that time of Cathal's arrival it was a place of great darkness and sin.

As Cathal approached the gates of the town there was a blind man begging outside. He stopped to speak to the man and, finding him open to the message, proceeded to instruct him in Christ's teaching. As he listened the blind man's heart was opened to the message he heard; so too were his eyes and he could see again. Over the next few years Cathal converted the town. It was not an easy task; the people had been hardened by years of war and corruption and they were wary of strangers with foreign accents, but his dedication, words and miracle working won them over in the end.

Cathal lived for many years as Bishop of Taranto. When he felt death was near, he gathered his bishops around him and warned them to be ready for those who would try to undo all the work he had done. His request to be buried in Taranto was honoured and his tomb is in the great cathedral that bears his name in its Italian form, '*Cathaldus*'. Today the town still remember St Cathaldus, the Irish man shipwrecked on their shore, who brought Christianity to their town. There are numerous churches bearing his name, not only in that vicinity but all across southern Italy and into parts of Greece as well. They pray to him to calm storms and avert droughts, and a three-day celebration is held from 8–10 May each year in his honour, celebrated in Bologna, Cremona, Genoa, Mantua, Rimini, Sicily and Verona too.

St Ailbhe (died 528): Feast Day 12 September

St Ailbhe's father ran away before Ailbhe was born, for fear of the local king. The king had forbade the union between the mother and father and now ordered that the child be killed. The servants, though, hadn't the heart to do such a thing as murder a child, so they left him on a rock to the mercy of the elements and wild animals. As it turned out, when his own people had deserted him a she-wolf came to his rescue and nursed him and cared for him.

After some time, a passing man came across the child and took him in. He and his family were from Britain but living in Ireland at that time. They had decided to return to their own country and they had intended to leave Ailbhe behind, but they found that on the day they planned to cross the sea they couldn't; the seas were too rough. Not until they promised to bring Ailbhe with them did the seas calm enough that they could make the crossing.

Later Ailbhe made his way from Britain to Gaul (France) and on to Rome where he studied to become a priest and later was made a bishop before returning to Ireland to make the people of Ireland 'not just Christians but Saints'.

One day Ailbhe's peace was disturbed when a she-wolf burst in on him, chased by a hunting party. She approached Ailbhe and laid her head on his breast. Ailbhe recognised her to be the same she-wolf who had nursed him. He granted her protection and from that day on she and her cubs ate at his table.

Ailbhe set up a monastery and school in *Imleach Iubhair*, 'border of the lake of yew trees', now known as Emly. Emly was one of the oldest and most important monastic sites in Ireland and the seat of the dioscese up to the gifting of Cashel to the Church.

One of the many pupils Ailbhe had at Emly was St Enda. After a time, Enda wished to go away and set up his own monastery and so Ailbhe petitioned Aengus, the first Christian king of Munster, for some land for Enda to build his monastery on. That night, the king dreamt of islands off the coast of his territories which he had not known about before. These were the Aran Islands, and he granted them to Enda. The ruins of the great monastery Enda built there can still be seen on Inismor today.

Ailbhe spent time in Wales where he baptised St David who became the patron saint of Wales. He is remembered there as St Elvis – the anglicised form of Ailbhe. Ailbhe himself is the patron saint of the Dioscese of Emly and Cashel, as well as the patron saint of wolves.

St Crónán of Roscrea (died 640): Feast Day 28 April

St Crónán was the son of Odhran and born in the Barony of Ely O'Carroll in Offaly. His mother was Coemri, from County Clare, and Crónán spent a great deal of his youth there. As a young man he journeyed with Mobhi and Mochoinne, the sons of his mother's sister. They visited many holy houses to be taught there before heading out themselves to each leave their mark on the spiritual lives of communities in Ireland. Crónán is said to have founded nearly fifty monasteries but the most famous was at Roscrea.

Around 610 he returned to his home area and built a monastery at Seanross, also known as Monahincha, a lonely wild area in a wooded land near the now dried-up lake – Lough Crea. Crónán wanted to be hospitable man – he was generous and enjoyed company – but his settlement was far off the beaten track. There is a story that one time two men were travelling from Limerick to Dublin and, being near to Crónán's settlement, thought to spend the night there, but they got lost in the wooded area and ended up spending the night out of doors. When Crónán heard about this he was distressed, so he moved the monastery to be closer to the great road – *Slighe Dala*, one of the five main routes which left from the Hill of Tara to the corners of Ireland. The *Sligh Dala* went from Tara all the way to County Kerry.

In the woods of Cre (named after the wife of Dala), in Irish *Ross Cré* (Roscrea), Crónán built his monastery and school. His generosity and hospitality were known far and wide and there are many stories of a miraculous generosity. One story tells that one time Crónán, finding himself short of beer for his guests, he prayed and lo, there was enough beer and more for everyone present. The busy town of Roscrea soon built up around the monastery.

Another time St Crónán needed a bible for his school. He asked Dimma, a talented scholar and transcriber, to copy out the four gospels for him. Dimma said he could only afford to give one day to such a task which would be near impossible to complete in that time frame.

'That's OK,' said Crónán, 'But begin now and don't stop until sunset.' Dimma set to work, copied out the four gospels and illustrated them with four beautiful pictures. It took forty days for Dimma to complete the task but in all that time the sun did not set, leaving Dimma to believe he had done it in one day. This miracle became known as the miracle of Crónán.

Later in the eleventh and twelfth century Tathen O'Carroll, chieftain of the area, had an ornate case made to house the book. The Book of Dimma is one of the ten sacred manuscripts written in Ireland before the year 1000 AD. It is housed and can be viewed today in Trinity College.

Crónán died a blind hermit around the 10 May 640 and is buried on the grounds of his cathedral. The field opposite St Crónán's school in Longfordwood was known as the 'Church Field' and it was believed that St Crónán had a chapel here. In the burial grounds of that chapel there was a stone with a hollow in it which never dried out and always had water in it. The water was known to cure warts up to the 1930s anyway, if not still today.

St Rudhán of Derrynaflan (died 584): Feast Day 5 April

Diarmuid Mac Cerbhaill was the last pagan king of Ireland. During his reign he frequently fell into argument with the clerics and holy men of the time; it was he who judged in St Finnian's favour when St Columba copied one of Finnian's books without permission. Diarmuid ruled, 'To every cow its calf, to every book its copy', which led to a great battle known as the 'Battle of the Books' – Diarmuid lost.

Diarmuid had a druid called Bec Mac De, by all historical accounts a great seer. He told Diarmuid that he would die by the hand of his foster brother, Aodh Dubh. So, Diarmuid duly banished Aodh from the kingdom.

At that time a person in fear of their life could go to a monastery for sanctuary and it was expected that if they did so all persons would respect the sanctuary given. Diarmuid at that time had a man in his service who was mean and disrespectful. Aodh Guaire from Connacht killed him and ran to St Rudhán for protection and sanctuary, in fear of Diarmuid. St Rudhán granted him sanctuary and hid him in one of his monasteries.

But Dairmuid went to the monastery and questioned St Rudhán.

'Where is Aodh?' asked Diarmuid, knowing St Rudhán couldn't tell a lie.

'I don't know, unless he is under where you are standing?' answered the saint. Diarmuid was nearly ready to walk away but he came back and searched under the place where he had been standing, found Aodh hiding there and took him away in violation of the sanctuary St Rudhán had granted.

St Rudhán was not pleased. He followed Diarmuid to Tara where they argued. Diarmuid cursed Rudhán that his monasteries would lie wasted and vacant; Rudhán cursed Diarmuid and prophesied that Diarmuid would be killed by a falling beam from the roof of his great hall in Tara. In the end Diarmuid released Aodh and Rudhán left.

Diarmuid had the beam removed from his hall in Tara and thrown in the sea. He then asked Bec, his own druid, for the manner of his death. Bec told him it would be a threefold death: slaughter, burning and drowning on a night when he wore a linen shirt woven from flax grown from a single seed, and drank ale brewed from a single grain and ate pork from a sow that had never farrowed (had piglets). Diarmuid dismissed the prophecies and went on about his business.

The roof beam was retrieved from the sea by Banbán and worked into the roof of his hall at Rath Beg in County Antrim. Banbán invited Diarmuid to dine with him and Diarmuid accepted. During the evening he was given ale to drink, pork to eat and that night he was given a linen nightshirt to sleep in. Banban's daughter told Diarmuid that the shirt had been woven from flax grown from a single seed, that the ale had been brewed from grain coming from a single grain and that the pork had come from a sow who had never farrowed. Diarmuid realised that the prophecy was coming true and tried to leave. But Aed Dubh was also in Banbán's house that night and he was waiting, sword in hand. He smote Diarmuid a blow and then set the room on fire. Diarmuid climbed into the ale barrel to escape the fire. The beam in the roof (the one which Diarmuid had cut from his hall and thrown in the sea) fell and hit Diarmuid, killing him.

Thus did the prophecy come true. Diamuid was killed by Aodh Dubh, killed by the falling beam, and suffered a death of slaughter, fire and drowning.

Aodh himself went on to suffer a prophesied death of falling from wood into water – he was killed on a ship.

DERRYNAFLAN

Doire na Flan (Derrynaflan) means the 'wood of the Flans'. Flan is a term for a flaming red-haired person and the Flans referred to are Flan, son of Fairchellaig, who became Abbot of Lismore, and Flan, son of Dubh Tuinne of Dairinis, both of whom lived around the 820s. It was not they, however, who built nor founded the monastery. The monastery of Derrynaflan was founded some 300 years previously by Rudhán of Lorrh. Derrynaflan Island is not your typical island surrounded by water. It is a little island of green in Kileens bog near Killenaule in County Tipperary. The name may sound familiar because one of the most important finds ever made in the

country was made there in the 1980, known as the Derrynaflan Horde which includes the Derrynaflan Chalice and Patten can be viewed at the National Museum of Ireland on Kildare Street, Dublin.

The bog around the island is harvested now, but centuries ago you would have thought the place an isolated spot. Still there is evidence of roadways leading from the island out, though not all of them sprang miraculously from the bog itself as in St Colmán's case.

St Colmán of Daire Mór (Durrihy North of Thurles) was bringing a gift of butter to St Rudhán in Derrynaflan. The butter was in a vessel carried by two oxen. The road from Durrihy to Derrynaflan crossed the bog and was difficult, well really there was no road to follow, just a track. A lone person would have no trouble but the two oxen were getting caught in the mud and boggy ground and the going was very difficult. Miraculously a road sprang up out of the bog enabling Colmán to complete his journey to his friend and deliver the promised butter.

ST CUALAN OF KILCUILAN: FEAST DAY 18 FEBRUARY

The Derrynaflan horde wasn't the only saintly treasure found in Tipperary. In the hollow of a tree in Kilcuilan a bell was found, a very old bell known as *Bearnan Cuailan.*

St Cualan came to Tipperary in the seventh century and built a monastery at Gleann Caoin, known today as Glenkeen. Just across the valley his followers built a church which carried his name, Kilcuilan. St Cualan is referred to in European texts as one of the most noted saints of the early church.

One of the artefacts associated with St Cualan is the bell, *Bearnan Cuailan.* During the penal times, when priests were hunted and killed, the bell must have been hidden in the tree and centuries later was rediscovered. The bell is said to have peculiar properties in that it caused liars to fall into convulsions and slowly strangled them if hung around their necks.

The bell is now on view in the British Museum and a replica can be seen in Borrisoleigh church.

Sources

Saints of Tipperary: www.omniumsanctorumhiberniae.blogspot. ie; local websites for Derrynaflan, Emly, Clogheen and Taranto, wikepidia

St Cronan: NFC Schools Vol.549: Scoil an Clochar, Roscrea, Barony of Ikerrin, Tipperary, pp.79–82, Emir O'Berine, and pp.96–100, Emily O'Carroll; NFC Schools Vol.547 Clonmore School, Killavinogue, Ikerrins, p.210, 'St Cronan' Maud Treacy from Bartly Maher, age 75; www.omniumsanctorumhiberniae.blogspot.ie

St Rudhán: www.lorrhadorrha.ie www.omniumsanctorumhiberniae.blogspot.ie

6

PLACES OF TIPPERARY

One of the most fascinating parts of working on a collection like this is finding the stories behind place names. These are only some of the stories of how different places in Tipperary got their names. There are many, many, more hinted at in each signpost and town plaque.

CLOUGHJORDAN

Cloughjordan, *Cloch Suirdan* in Irish, translates as the Stone of Jordan. De Marisco, the Norman settler who founded the town, had been to the Holy Land as part of the Crusades and brought back a stone from the River Jordan. The stone was built into the doorway of his castle giving the place the name Stone of Jordan, *cloch* being the Irish word for stone.

HOLY CROSS ABBEY

Holy Cross Abbey is so named because it has a relic of the true cross on which Jesus Christ was crucified.

The story is that 'Pierce the fair', son of Isabelle of Angoule, was collecting the Peter's Pence collection in the area of Holy

Cross Abbey. He was attacked, robbed and murdered and his body was left in a wood, in a shallow grave. No one knew what had happened to him or where he was, though it was presumed he was dead. Poor Isabelle, his mother, was stricken with grief.

An abbot in the local monastery had a dream of the body lying unclaimed in the woods. He followed the directions of the dream to the place he had seen and uncovered the body of the young man. He brought the body back to the monastery and buried it in a proper grave with the proper funeral rites.

Pierce was the son of Isabelle of Angouleme's second marriage. Her first marriage had been to King Henry II of England. After the death of Henry, she had returned to France and married Hugh X of Lusigan. The murder of her son upset her terribly but she was deeply grateful to the abbey for giving her son a proper burial.

As a token of her gratitude she bestowed on the abbey a relic of the true cross. The abbey became known as Holy Cross Abbey and thousands of pilgrims came to the abbey to pray before the relic.

Thieves may have been a cause of the relic coming to the abbey in 1233 but they were almost the cause of the relic being lost. In October 2011 two masked men came to the abbey one afternoon and took the relic from its case. Luckily though it was later found and returned to the abbey.

COLLETT'S LANE CLONMEL

In the 1690s Ireland was in the middle of a war between two kings: King James II was a Catholic and had a good following here in Ireland known as the Jacobites; his son-in-law, William of Orange, was a Protestant and the preferred king for the English. The two brought their differences to Ireland and fought their final battle on Irish soil on the banks of the River Boyne in

County Louth. However, for the years before, and I suppose you could say for years after, the differences between the two sides could be felt.

Mr Collett was a merchant who lived in Clonmel. At the time James II was still the rightful, if not disputed, king of England and Ireland. Tensions were high and the Battle of the Boyne was looming. Some could see what was ahead and Mr Collett was visited unexpectedly by the steward of Lord Caher.

'I have come to pay the debt of my master in the good and lawful money of his majesty King James.'

Now you might think this is a good thing, but the 'good and lawful money of King James' which Lord Caher's steward referred to were copper tokens which, by King James' law, were to pass for half crowns and shillings but which, in truth, were not nearly as valuable. The steward had come with four horsemen each laden with the copper tokens in order to pay the debt. By law the merchant had to accept them, but he knew if he did he'd never get the value of the debt he was owed.

He put on his best face. 'It's near dinner hour,' he said, 'you and your men must be weary and hungry, come and dine with me'. The riders and steward readily agreed and so they sat to dinner.

Collett tried to make the meal last as long as possible, trying to put off the inevitable transaction. However, every meal must eventually come to an end and so did this one. The steward was anxious to conclude his business and go his way, so Mr Collett told him to bring in the copper tokens so he could count them and make sure all was in order.

The four horsemen brought in the copper tokens and Collett began the job of counting them, but he counted the money in a clumsy fashion, making mistakes and having to restart again and again. Eventually though he could drag out the business no longer. He was resigning himself to the fact that he would have to accept the copper tokens and accept the loss of the debt when a clatter of horse's hooves was heard in the lane; a horseman arrived, sweaty and exhausted, and burst into the room breathless. He handed Mr Collett a letter. M. Collett read it and then smiled. He turned to the steward and said, 'Put your money back in your bags again and go and tell your master that my King has beaten his King.'

For that day was 2 July 1690, the day after the Battle of the Boyne where King James II had been defeated, so his money need no longer be accepted as the legal tender.

Note: Although the Battle of the Boyne is now commemorated on 12 July, it was held on 1 July 1690. The shift in the date is due to the changeover from the Julian calendar to the Gregorian calendar. In Ireland, the Gregorian calendar was adopted in 1752 and 14 September followed 2 September.

LOUGH DERG

The full name is Lough Dergheirc and means the lake of the bloody eye.

There was a king named Eochy Mac Luchta; he had only one eye, having lost the other in battle. He was a king known for his hospitality and generosity. One day, the poet Aithirne came by. Now in those days, as mentioned earlier, poets were very powerful people; if you upset them they could write a poem about you which could be the end of you. But some of them could abuse their position and demand of their patrons more than they could give. Eochy was known never to refuse a request and Aithirne took advantage of that.

So when Eochy asked what Aithirne would like for his poetry, Aithirne asked for his one remaining eye. Without hesitation Eochy plucked it out and gave it to the poet. Aithirne took the eye to the lake to wash the blood off and the lake turned red and so Eochy said 'let this lake be called Loch Dergdheirc – the lake of the bloody eye.' Eochy was rewarded for his generosity and both his eyes were miraculously returned to him. There is a great version of this story in the *Clare Folk Tales* book as both Clare and Tipperary share Lough Derg as a boundary between them.

CASTLETOWN GRAVEYARD

There was a time when a servant was little more than a slave to his master. They were expected to do as they were told without question, go where they were sent and take on whatever task they were given – if they didn't it was quite acceptable for them to be physically punished for their disobedience or laziness.

There was a chieftain near Castletown one time who beat his servant so badly that the poor man died as a result. Time went by and the chieftain began to feel sorry for his crime. His conscience troubled him until he at last visited a holy man and told him his worries. The holy man told him to arise early the next morning and prepare for a journey. He would find a little white horse saddled and waiting for him outside the castle and tied to the stirrups of the horse there would be a little bag of sand. The chieftain was to get on the horse and head off, but keep an eye on the little bag of sand. Wherever the bag fell off there he was to build a church in atonement for his sin.

The chieftain got up in the morning and there was the horse waiting for him outside the door and the little bag of sand tied to the stirrups. He got up on the horse and headed off, keeping an eye on the little bag of sand. Eventually it fell off the stirrup. On that spot the church was built and a graveyard grew up around it which is where Castletown graveyard is now. In the graveyard there is still the ruins of an old church, all covered with ivy now, but made of the very stones that chieftain used to build the original church.

NEW TIPPERARY

In the 1880s, while the county of Tipperary struggled with their landlords in their own way, the town of Tipperary took its own stand. The local landlord, Arthur Smith Barry, was deeply involved in the landlords' counterstand to the tenants' Plan of Campaign. This campaign involved tenants standing together to ask for lower rents when harvests were poor and, if refused, they withheld the rent from the landlord, but paid it to a central fund to support evicted tenants and those falling on hard times. When Arthur Smith Barry evicted tenants in Cork the tenants in Tipperary, in solidarity, stopped paying their rent. Many were evicted, both tenants and businessmen, so they took themselves and their business outside the town and built a 'New Tipperary' and carried on their business there.

Eventually, there was an agreement between the tenants and Barry and they moved back to the old town. The area where Dillon Street and Emmet Street are in Tipperary Town today is where the 'New Tipperary stood'.

LOUGHMOE: PURCELL COAT OF ARMS

Just outside Thurles stands the castle of Loughmoe. The present castle has stood there since the 1300s, but the land name – *Luach Magh* (field of reward) – and the legend, implies that there was a castle there from long before. The legend tells the story of how the Purcell family earned their coat of arms.

The King of Loughmoe and his people were terrorised and tormented by a wild boar and his sow. So feared was this wild boar that the king offered a reward – his daughter's hand in marriage, the castle and land – to anyone who could rid the land of the boar.

Many young men came, whether through love of the king's daughter or the wish for the land, and tried their luck at slaying the boar but all met the same gruesome end.

Along came a man by the name of Purcell and he asked the king for his turn in seeking and killing the boar. The king gave him permission to try but without much hope of seeing him succeed.

At that time, Loughmoe and much of its neighbouring parishes were covered in an ash wood and it was said that the trees of the wood were so close together that it would be possible to step from branch to branch and cross the parish through the trees without ever setting a foot to the ground. Into the forest went Purcell, but not by the paths of the wood; he strode from branch to branch in the top of the trees. Purcell had been told by some of the king's servants that the boar that day was away north in the wood and that the sow was closer to them in a quiet spot with her *bonamhs* (piglets). Purcell decided to try get rid of the sow and her young first. He moved through the branches and, when he came in sight of the sow, lifted his bow and arrows and took aim. He showered arrows down on that sow but her hide was so thick none of them penetrated. The sow rose from her spot, livid at the attack and, sensing Purcell in the trees, made for them to knock him out. The sow at the foot of the tree looked up at Purcell, grunting and snorting. At one time when her mouth was opened wide, Purcell sent an arrow down her throat and the sow, giving a last awful grunt, keeled over dead.

The boar on the other side of the wood heard the death cry of his mate. He made his way through the trees, parting the ash trees as if they were grass. When he came to the corpse of the dead sow he went wild, stood on his hind legs against the tree, swaying it to and fro in an effort to uproot it. Purcell, having learned from the experience with the sow, bided his time till the boar for a moment exposed his jaws and mouth and Purcell could send an arrow through them. The arrow went through the boar's mouth and he sped off in great pain to die in a place the far side of Thurles.

Purcell married the king's daughter and came to live in the castle where Purcells have had a presence ever since. The story of the killing of the wild boar, the sow and her *bonamhs* is to be seen in the Purcell coat of arms which has four boar's heads.

LONDERGAN THE LOUGHMOE HURLER

At the Templemore side of Loughmoe castle there was an embankment which was said to be the 'grand stand' to the Purcell hurling Field. Apparently the family so loved the sport they had their own field with the embankment built for watching matches, and their own team to boot.

This private team was made up of the very best of hurlers, and one worth noting was a man by the name of Londergan. Londergan would stand at one side of the castle and hit a ball high over the roof, then he would race to the other side of the castle to hit the ball before it reached the ground, back over the castle and then race back to do the same again; nine times he was known to have hit the ball thus over and back across the castle, without letting it hit the ground.

But good and all as Londergan was, as a player he had two faults: the first that he was quarrelsome and never seemed to play a match without starting some argument or fight; and secondly that he never could stay to his part of the pitch. He had to be where the ball was – a manager's nightmare.

On this particular occasion there was a big match coming up and the baron of the castle at the time thought it might go better if Londergan was not there to play. So, he sent Londergan on a message, to deliver a letter to Dublin, on foot, 90 miles away ensuring he couldn't be there to play the game.

Now Londergan was no fool and when on Friday – the day before the match – he was set the task to deliver the letter to Dublin he knew it was to keep him from the match. However, he would not refuse a message his master sent him on so he set off at a brisk pace to Dublin to deliver the letter. Londergan kept his pace all the way to Dublin, he delivered the letter, took the reply and set off back to Loughmoe. He walked so fast that he was back by early Saturday afternoon, just in time for the start of the match.

When Baron Purcell saw him he was furious. 'I sent you to deliver a letter,' he said, 'Why didn't you go?'

'I did go,' replied Londergan, 'And to prove it, here's your reply.' And he produced the answer to the letter he had received in Dublin. When Purcell saw the reply he realised what Londergan had done, he ordered that Londregan be striped and placed in a barrel of butter to stop his joints from stiffening up because of the exerting walk.

They say that the heat from Londergan after his 'brisk' walk was so great he melted right through the butter to the bottom of the barrel. Maybe he got a spot in that important hurling game after all, but I think the feat of walking the 90 miles to Dublin and back again in twenty-four hours enough to earn Londergan a claim to fame.

Sources
Collett's Lane Clonmel: *My Clonmel Scrap Book*
Castletown Graveyard Source: NFC Schools Vol.548, Scoil Lios Dubh, Dún Chiarán, Ikerrin, pp.2–3 'Castletown Graveyard' from William McCormack died 1929
New Tipperary Sources: NFC 548 pp.2–3 from William MacCormack, Lisduff, Moneygall
Loughmoe-Purcell Coat of Arms and Londergan the Loughmoe Hurler: 'Loughmoe Castle and its Legends' by Revd St John D. Seymore, *The Journal of the Royal Society of Antiquaries of Ireland*, Fifth Series, Vol.39, no.1 (1908), pp.70–74

7

PEOPLE OF
TIPPERARY

There have been many notable people from County Tipperary who have left their mark in sports, music, politics and history. Every community has its sons and daughters who they celebrate and of whom they are proud. Here are a few of the names you might be familiar with but maybe didn't realise came from Tipperary.

DR GEOFFREY KEATING –
IRISH HISTORIAN 1570–1650

In researching this book I've read through the old manuscripts many times (now digitally available online through CELT). One of the manuscripts I have most often visited is Geoffrey Keating's *History of Ireland*. For some of us there are places we pass everyday, never wondering or asking about the things that have happened there; streets we live on, never asking who they are named after; and works we read, never wondering about who wrote them.

Foras Feasa ar Éirinn is a history of old Ireland, telling of the kings and battles and mythology. I wish it had been a textbook when I was at school because I would never have left it down. I have been diverted so many times in researching, just to follow through on an interesting thread of something which had nothing to do with what I opened the pages for originally, but did I ever ask who Geoffery Keating was, when he lived or where he came from?

Well ... Geoffrey Keating (Seathrun Ceitinn) was born in the town land of Burgess, near Clogheen, in 1570. He entered the priesthood, was ordained in France and returned to Ireland to his native parish in 1610, where he built a church in Tubrid, not far from the great moat of Knockgraffon. He was an Irish speaker as was the norm in those years, but more than that, Keating has been described as the 'greatest master and best model of Irish prose'. The 1600s were not a good time to be Catholic. Keating worked away without much trouble for a number of years but then he had to go on the run. He went into hiding in a cave in the glen of Aherlow and it is there that he worked on his great work *Foras Feasa an Eireann*, 'The History of Ireland'.

In 1650 Keating was killed by a Cromwellian soldier and was buried in his church at Tubrid.

Charles J. Kickham – Fenain Leader and Author 1828–1882

Charles J. Kickham was a Fenian Leader, born in 1828 in Mullinahone. He was a good scholar and it was hoped he might go on to be a doctor, but an accident with gunpowder put an end to that dream, permanently damaging his sight and hearing. In the 1830s Charles' father was involved with the tithe wars. Charles himself was much influenced by the ideas of the Young Irelanders and was part of a local group until the events of 1848 in Ballingarry forced him into hiding.

In 1855 he joined the Fenians and travelled to America, where many of the leaders were. He rose through the ranks and sat on the executive council alongside Stephens Luby and O'Leary. He wrote articles for the *Irish People*, a newspaper he later edited. Back in Ireland in 1865, Kickham was arrested when police raided the premises of the paper. By this time he was almost completely blind. He spent four years in prison in England for writing 'treasonous' articles. After his release he continued his involvement at a very high level in the Irish Republican Brotherhood and the fight for independence. He wrote many articles, novels and ballads. He died in 1882 and nearly 10,000 people followed his funeral to Heuston Station before he was brought to his home town of Mullinahone, where he is buried.

One of Kickham's most famous songs is 'Slievenamon', which has become the unofficial anthem of County Tipperary, sung at many of the sporting events.

Slievenamon

Alone, all alone, by the wave-washed strand,
All alone in the crowded hall.
The hall it is gay and the waves they are grand
But my heart is not there at all.
It flies far away, by night and by day
To the times and the joys that are gone.
But I never can forget the sweet maiden I met
In the valley of Slievenamon.

It was not the grace of her queenly air
Nor the cheeks of the roses glow,
Her soft dark eyes or her curly hair,
Nor was it her lily white brow.
'Twas the soul of truth and of melting ruth,
And a smile like the summer's day.
That stole my heart away on that bright summer's day
In the valley of sweet Slievenamon.

In the festive ball and the wave-washed shore
My restless spirit cries –
'My land, oh my land, shall I never see you more,
My country will you never up-rise?
By night and by day I will ever, ever pray,
As darkly my life it rolls on,
To see our flag unrolled and my true love unfold
In the valley near Slievenamon.

Charles Bianconi – Entrepreneur (1786–1875)

Carlo Bianconi was born in Italy in 1786. Those were turbulent times with Napoleon on the rise, and Bianconi, seeing what might lie ahead, left Italy and came west. He came to Ireland in 1802 and settled in Tipperary. He is best remembered for the Bianconi coaches which ran on many of the national routes, taking people from one place to another. There was even a system of inns along the route where people could stop for a night on their journey.

In the 1850s, with the coming of the steam train, the coaches continued to do well, offering a link system between train and coach which people could use to get from one place to another, one of the first ever integrated public transport systems. Some of the Bianconi Inns are still operational: you can visit them in Bianconi Inn, Killorglin, County Kerry, and Anthony's Inn, Pilltown, County Kilkenny, though the coach system is no longer in use. Bianconi died in 1875 and is buried in his local church of Boherlahan to which he donated the land for it to be built.

Maurice Davin – Sportsman (1842–1927)

Maurice Davin was born in Carrick-on-Suir in 1842. He grew to 6ft 1in in height and weighed 15 stone. During the 1870s it was said no man could come near him in throwing. On 5 June 1876, he got to prove this when he set a record for the hammer throw at the very first international teams event held in Lansdowne Road Park between England and Ireland. Maurice is recorded as being the very first person to represent Ireland at an international event. Of the fourteen events held, England won nine and Ireland five. Three of those events were won by the Davin brothers, Maurice winning the shot put and hammer throw, and Pat and Tom, his brothers, sharing first place for the high jump.

In 1884, Maurice read 'A Word about Irish Athletics' in the *United Ireland* and *Irishman*, a letter written anonymously by Michael Cusack. Michael called on the Irish people to take charge of their own games, particularly those games peculiar to the Irish. Maurice replied to the letter, agreeing in principle with what Michael said though there were a few comments of Cusack's which he didn't agree with.

This led to a meeting being called in Hayes Commercial Hotel, Thurles, on 1 November 1884 from which was born the Gaelic Athletic Association. Maurice Davin was elected the first President of the organisation and Michael Cusack, Secretary.

Thomas Croke, Archbishop of Cashel, Charles Stewart Parnell, and Mr Michael Davitt became patrons to the organisation. Murice Davin died in 1927, aged eighty-five.

PATRICK SHEEHAN

Patrick Sheehan came from the Glen of Aherlow and joined the British Army. He was sent to the Crimea in 1854 where he took part in the Siege of Sebastopol in September 1855, the final chapter in the Crimean War. He was blinded and sent home on an army pension but the pension he got only lasted nine months and by 1857 Patrick was begging on the streets. That same year, he was arrested for begging on Grafton Street. The story was circulated through the

papers and caused outrage. The incident was popularised by Charles
J. Kickham's ballad, 'The Ballad of Patrick Sheehan' (also known as
the 'Glen of Aherlow'), which also worked as an anti-recruitment
song. The British Government were shamed into intervening in
Patrick's case and he received a pension for life of a shilling a day.

The Ballad of Patrick Sheehan / Glen of Aherlow

My name is Patrick Sheehan, and my years are thirty-four;
Tipperary is my native place, not far from Galtymore;
I came of honest parents, but now they're lying low;
Though' many's the pleasant days we spent in the Glen of Aherlow.

My father died; I closed his eyes, outside the cabin door;
For the landlord and the sheriff too, were there the day before,
And then my lovin' mother, and my sisters three, also,
Were forced to go with broken hearts, from the Glen of Aherlow

For three long months, in search of work, I wandered far and near;
I then went to the poorhouse to see my mother dear;
The news I heard near broke my heart, but still in all my woe,
I blessed the friends who made their graves in the Glen of Aherlow.

Bereft of home and kith and kin, with plenty all around,
I starved within my cabin, and slept upon the ground;
But cruel as my lot was, I never did hardship know,
Till I joined the English army, far away from Aherlow.

'Rouse up there,' cried the corporal, 'Ya lazy Irish hound!
Why don't you hear the bugle, its call to arms to sound?'
I found I had been dreaming of the days long, long ago,
And I woke upon Sebastopol, and not in Aherlow.

I tried to find my musket, how dark I thought the night!
O blessed God! It wasn't dark, it was the broad daylight!
And when I found that I was blind, my tears began to flow,
And I longed for even a pauper's grave in the Glen of Aherlow.

A poor neglected mendicant, I wander Dublin's streets
My nine months' pension it being out, I beg from all I meet;
As I joined my country's tyrants, my face I can never show,
Amongst my dear old neighbours in the Glen of Aherlow.

So Irish youths, dear countrymen, take heed in what I say;
For if you join the English ranks, you'll surely rue the day
And whenever you're tempted, a-soldiering to go.
Remember poor blind Sheehan from the Glen of Aherlow.

8

JOSEPH DAMER

Joseph Damer was born in 1630 in England. He served under Cromwell, and came to Ireland with him. Damer received lands in Shronel in Tipperary and left such an impression on the area and people that he has slipped into the folklore. The following are just a sample of the some of the stories about him to be found in the National Folklore Collection.

Damer was was a stockbroker in Dublin and a land owner in Shronel. He was a rich and successful man. He had gold in his vaults in Shronel and was always building new rooms and extensions for his grand castle. But Damer had not always been a rich man. This is the story of how he got his money.

When Cromwell came to Ireland he brought everything he might need with him, so not only did his army have soldiers, it also had craftspeople with the various skills that might be necessary: gun makers, tailors, carpenters, cloth makers etc.

Damer was a chandler and he used to follow the army making tallow candles.

When Cromwell came near Hoar Abbey the monks had already evacuated. The monastery had a lot of gold and when they heard Cromwell was coming they put the gold in firkins, melted tallow down over them and left them in the vaults. When Cromwell came, all he could find of any worth was the firkins of tallow which he

ordered to be given to his chandler – well why not? He'd get a few candles out of it anyway.

Damer took the firkins, opened them and began using the tallow to make candles. Soon he came to the gold coins stashed underneath. He hid them away until times got quiet, and then used them on the stock exchange. He bought out nearly all of west Tipperary as far as you can see from the hill of Shronel, and deposited the rest of his gold in the vaults of the old castle there.

LIAM *DALL* HEFFERNON – BLIND HEFFERNON

Liam *Dall* (blind) Heffernon was a weaver who lived in Shronel. He was also known as a bard who composed songs and poems and was a man of some influence. He had been educated in Louvain in France, but he had returned home when his eyesight began to fail (either due to having had smallpox or from cataracts). It gradually got worse from then on, though he was old before he lost it completely. Liam didn't get on that well with Damer, and he would compose songs and poems about Damer's miserliness. Mind you, that didn't stop Liam going up to the mansion for his dinner every now and then.

At one time there were two Scotsmen who worked for Damer, Barlow and Butler. Barlow was a Irish speaker and often Liam and he would speak in Irish. One day when Liam went to the mansion, Barlow met him at the door. 'Take your time,' said Barlow in Irish, 'There's a big crowd of men there, you'll get nothing at present.'

'Who's there?' asked Liam

'There's Lowe of Kilshane and Roe of Rossborogh and Mr Damer himself is at home.'

'My good man,' said Liam, 'there'll come a day when there won't be a Damer there, nor a Lowe in Kilashane nor a Roe of Rosborough, but there'll always be a Heffernan of Shronel.'

Damer wanted to know what Liam had been saying but he didn't understand the Irish so he asked Barlow.

'What has the old bard been saying?'

Quickly Barlow answered, 'He says that Damer has a great table and may it always be there,' answered Barlow.

'Oh, go give him his dinner,' replied Damer.

Another time Liam Dall (before he went blind) got caught up with the priest hunting. There had been a Tipperary priest captured in Cashel. He was being taken by cart to Limerick and as they passed through each little village, the soldiers would throw the priest out of the cart and drag him, tied by the shoulders, through the streets of the village, then load him back in the cart till they got to the next village. This carried on till they came to Tipperary town and there again they pitched off the priest. The Irish people were following behind in a mob, but they kept well back out of fear. Liam Dall wasn't a Catholic but the activity brought him out of his house.

'Well,' said he to the Catholic crowd, 'Isn't he your pastor?'

'He is,' said the people.

'If he were my pastor,' said Heffernan, 'I'd loose the last drop of my blood before I'd allow him to be dragged like that.'

'That's what we're here for,' said one of the crowd, 'but we've no leader.'

'I'll lead you,' said Heffernan, even though he was of a different religion.

After going through the town the soldiers hoisted the priest back on the cart until they reached the next village where they threw him off again. Then Liam ordered the people in on them. The whole crowd caught and jostled the soldiers and threw them into a big stone quarry below in Cullen, killing them and rescuing the priest.

There was a big law suit afterwards and about two or three parishes of people were wanted for the murder of the seven men, but it was such a complicated case that the judges couldn't make sense of it. Eventually the judges decided to leave the decision to a popular and well-respected man who would come and view all the suspects and state if they were present at the murders or not. Liam Dall was the chosen man and was brought to the court. Every man arrested by the soldiers was let by Liam and his decision as to whether the prisoner had been there or not was accepted by the judge.

Liam condemned no man, and the judge had to conclude that no man of those parishes had played any part in the murders and the trial was dismissed.

DAMER AND ENGLISH

Damer had a carter, a man named English. One day English saw a jackdaw rise out of a chimney of the castle with something shiny in its beak and drop it into the trunk of an old tree in the woods. English thought it was a gold coin, so he waited and watched for the jackdaw again. Sure enough, it came back out of the chimney in the castle with a gold coin which it dropped again into the old tree trunk. English then thought of a plan.

He broke the shaft of his cart, and went to Damer, 'Sir,' said he, 'I've broken the shaft of my cart.' And he asked for permission to cut a tree in the woods to use to make a new shaft.

'You may cut any tree you wish,' said Damer.

Damer asked English if he needed a man to help him. 'No,' said English, 'My son is a fine hardy lad, now he'll help me.'

English and his son went into the wood and cut the tree they had seen the jackdaw drop the coin into, sure enough there in the centre of the tree was a stash of golden coins. They brought away the stash and a few years later English bought a farm a few miles away near Longstone.

DAMER AND THE TAILOR

It was said that Damer wore plain clothes, never drawing any attention to his wealth, but his servants would be dressed in fine clothes with golden buttons and there would be little golden bells on the horses. Damer himself wore a plain cloak.

There was a tailor one time who made a suit of clothes for him and Damer was very pleased with his work.

'That pleases me,' said Damer, 'How much should I pay you?'

Now the tailor had heard stories of the Damer's horde of gold, though no one could say that they had seen it.

'You needn't pay me anything sir,' said the tailor, 'Just let me see your gold.'

'You want to see my wealth?'

Damer got his keys and brought the tailor through a corridor of the castle at Shronel. There were five metal doors, all locked. Damer opened one of the doors and the tailor saw the pile within, as big as five barrels of barley.

Damer showed the tailor all five rooms and they were all the same with piles of gold on the floor.

'I've seen enough,' said the tailor.

'And what good has it done you?' asked Damer

'As much as it does you; you can only look at it and now I've done that too.'

'Stoop down,' said Damer, 'and take as much as you can scoop in your two hands,'

The tailor did so and went away rich and pleased.

Sources

Bealoideas, Iml 4 Uimhir 3 (1934), p.283 collected by Martin Burke from Thomas Power, NFC 700, pp.140–142 collected by Seosamh O'Dálaigh from Joe Fannin, age 79, Two-Mile-Borris

9

REBELS, RUFFIANS AND HARD TIMES

ABDUCTION OF ELEANOR ARBUTHNOT

The stories we most remember, I think, are not the wild fantastical ones of the imagination, but the almost unbelievably true ones. People over the centuries have done crazy things – mostly for love (or so they think). This must be one of the most crazy stories and I can't help wonder whether I should feel more sorry for the poor John Rutter Carden or Eleanor Arbuthnot.

John Rutter Carden lived in Barnane house, not far from Templemore. He was an interesting character. He had studied in England and when he came of age returned to Tipperary to take over the family estate, but he found that it was in debt. Many of his tenants had had years of no one collecting or making sure rents were paid and they had got into the habit of not paying. So, John gave an ultimatum: 'pay up or get out'. Many refused and planned to continue as they had, defying Carden to follow through on his threat. Carden said nothing but returned to the house in Barnane. He employed blacksmiths and carpenters to make the house into a fortress, with bullet-proof windows and cut away stairs so if the first floor was taken he could retreat to the second by pulling up a ladder.

On the occasion when a mob arrived to attack him in his house they found they could not get near him, so they brought a horse and plough and proceeded to plough up the lovely well-kept lawns at the front of the house. Carden fired a cannon at them and they cleared off. Court cases began, and tenants were evicted for non-payment of rents, but anyone who 'surrendered' was restored to their lands with favourable terms. Carden's pluck and courage during those years earned him the respect of friend and foe alike.

One story tells of him riding along toward Nenagh when he was shot at from behind a hedge. He turned his horse towards the hedge and cleared it with a jump then ran his assailants down, hitting one with his riding whip and catching the other. He brought them to Nenagh gaol where they were tried and hanged.

Down the other end of Tipperary, just a few miles outside Clonmel, is Rathroran Estate. There, in a big house, lived Captain George Gough and his wife. His wife's two sisters lived with them too, Laura and Eleanor Arbuthnot.

By all accounts they were beauties, especially Eleanor, who was eighteen years old and turned the head of many a young man. Among her admirers was our John Rutter Carden, who was in his fifties by this time. Carden had met Eleanor in the home of a neighbouring gentleman and had fallen hopelessly in love. He fancied that Eleanor loved him back. Wherever she was, there he was to be found too; flower shows, recitals, garden parties. It seemed as if he almost followed her around. Carden and Gough knew each other as gentlemen of that time would, through hunting parties and local affairs and were friendly enough, but the families were not particularly close.

Eventually Carden asked for Eleanor's hand, but she refused. Not only that, but her family refused and wrote to him asking him not to see Eleanor again. John Carden got it into his head that only for her family she would have accepted him.

He took every little encounter as confirmation of this, a shy turn of the head on the street, a glance in passing, and convinced himself that she did love him but was restrained by her family from showing it. The only solution was to remove her from the obstacle of her family.

Eleanor, Laura, their governess Miss Linden and Lady Gough attended services in the local church in Rathroran together on Wednesdays and Sundays.

On Sunday 2 July 1854, Mr Gough was away on business in Dublin. The ladies attended service as usual, but who was hanging about the church when they entered, only John Carden. When they were returning from church together, the carriage driver, Dwyer, noticed that Carden was following behind. As they approached the gates of Rathroran House, Dwyer saw a carriage and six horses waiting outside. There were six men nearby. Dywer felt that all was not right; he shook the reins and called to the horses to move on, but the six men stepped forward and caught the horses. Dwyer recognised one of them, 'Rainsborough you villain,' he called, but Rainsborough hit him a belt and Dwyer fell from the carriage. Then Rainsborough called to the other men to cut the reins and tackle of the horses.

Carden following behind, dismounted from his own horse and approached the carriage. Eleanor was sitting furthest into the carriage and Carden had to lean across Miss Linden to get near her. All the women in the carriage realised what was going on and they fought as best they could. Carden caught a hold of Elenor. Miss Lindon, sitting beside her, clenched her fist and hit Carden repeatedly until he began to bleed. Carden threw Miss Linden from the carriage and renewed his attempt to seize Eleanor.

Mrs Gough, whose health was not at its best, ran from the carriage up the avenue to the house calling for help. A local worker named McGrath was the first to hear and he called to the herdsman Smithwick to come quickly as 'murder was afoot'. While on another occasion the working 'peasantry' might be slow to interfere in a fight where a 'gentleman' was involved for fear they be brought to court, here was a case where women were being set upon. It was clear to McGrath and Smithwick who they should be defending and they had no scruples as to how hard they should hit.

Mrs Gough had run for help, Miss Linden had been thrown from the carriage, Eleanor's elder sister, Laura, was the last obstacle and she too was thrown from the carriage to the ground. Eleanor herself did not give up the fight; she put her arm through the halter in the carriage and held on for dear life, even though Carden pulled at her and grabbed at her and all but tore her from the carriage. None though fought like brave Miss Linden; repeatedly thrown to the ground she go back up and did all in her power to protect Eleanor from John Rutter Carden.

Carden, becoming frustrated, called to his helpers 'Cowards why don't you shoot?' for there were guns in the other carriage, but none but Rainsborough showed any willingness to proceed in that manner. They had been under the impression that Eleanor was a willing party in the abduction and, seeing now how things were, they realised that their own necks were on the line. Shouts could be heard from the house; help was coming. The men managed to convince Carden that his attempt was in vain and that it was time to fly. They got into the waiting carriage and set off at full speed on the road towards Templemore.

Carden had set up fresh horses at various stops between there and Galway where he had a boat waiting to take him and Eleanor – as he had thought – to Skye.

Clonmel was the first to raise the alarm and police there set off in hot pursuit. Meanwhile, a farm lad had rode to Cashel to raise the alarm there, where officer McCullough and the mounted police set off in pursuit. A few miles north of Holy Cross, near Farneybridge, they caught up with the carriage. McCullough called for them to stop and surrender but they shouted defiance, McCullough sprang from his horse, seized the reins of the carriage and ran it into the ditch. Carden and his men were captured and he was brought to Cashel Gaol.

When they went through the things in the carriage they found guns, money, wigs, a case of ladies clothes, blankets, two bottles of chloroform and instructions how to use it. Carden had planned to race through his own land, throwing a note to his servants telling them to lock the gates, delay pursuers and if possible lead them astray.

When news of the attempted abduction was first printed in the papers, people didn't believe it; they thought the era of abductions was long gone, but this story is a true one, and attracted great interest. So many people wished to be present at the court proceedings that there were whispers of it being held on the racecourse or fairgreen, but the judge would not consent to that. In the end John Rutter Carden got two years in prison for attempted abduction. You would think he learned his lesson, but no! Three years later Eleanor was staying with her sister in Dún Laoghaire when the house keeper reported that a strange woman had been calling, asking about Miss Eleanor and her movements. She later learned that the stranger was in the employment of Mr Carden and could promise the housekeeper a large sum of money if she would help set up a meeting between the two. The next time the woman called she was seized and passed over to the police. John Carden was bound to the peace and made to promise to leave Eleanor Arbuthnot alone.

He did leave her alone and he lived alone himself never marrying, and believing up to the last, some think, that Eleanor loved him.

Patrick Townsend

Patrick Townsend was a prominent Fenian who lived near Killaloe. One day, when he was coming home on horseback, he saw English soldiers approaching. Patrick was carrying arms and knew he would be shot if caught. He brought his horse in near the ditch and dropped the guns and arms into the ditch and continued on his journey past the soldiers. The soldiers had no idea what he had dropped into the ditch until they came near. Seeing the guns and arms, they turned and gave chase. Townsend turned up at Ballyclover cross and took to the fields. He came to the river which the horse refused to cross as it was too wide. Townsend got down off the horse, caught the saddle girth and ran his horse towards the river. He held on as the horse jumped and together they both made it to the other side.

On the other side Townsend stood defying the soldiers to cross; they couldn't and they had no authority to fire their own guns. One of the officers asked Townsend if he would sell his horse. Of course he did not and lived to fight another day, as they say.

Jerrie Grant

In olden days at Killavinogue near Templemore, there lived a highwayman by the name of Jerrie Grant. He used often call at Lidwell's in Dromard, which was also a favourite haunt of the English officers. Both parties were often there at the same time, but in separate apartments. One night the officers boasted of what they would do if ever Jerrie Grant were to cross their path. Lidwell, knowing Grant was in the building at the same time, slipped quietly from the soldiers and called at Grant's room. He told Grant what the officers had been saying.

'This very night,' said Grant, 'I will try their nerves.'

As Lidwell was leaving the room, Grant took off his pistols and left them with Lidwell.

'But what will you hold them up with?' asked Lidwell.

'Go out to your garden and get me a cabbage stump,' replied Grant.

'What do you want that for?' asked Lidwell

'To hold them up with of course,' was Grant's reply.

Lidwell went out to the garden and took a couple of stumps left after the cutting of the cabbage to Grant. Grant took these and went to lie in wait for the officers.

Eventually the officers left in high spirits, repeating again their threat that if they were to run into Jerrie Grant they would give him a 'hard knock'.

Grant was waiting down the avenue a few hundred metres from the house. As the officers rode past he called out, 'Stand and deliver,' at the same time stepping forward and pointing his cabbage stumps at them. 'I am Jerrie Grant.' Immediately the officers put up their hands, Grant took whatever money, gold, watches and guns they had and then told them to depart. Grant made his way back to Lidwell's and left him the money, gold, watches and guns he had taken from the officers then went on home himself.

The next day Lidwell rode to the military barracks to find out from the officers what had happened.

'What happened last night?' he asked.

The officers told how they had been held up by Grant and 'a hundred other men' who had robbed them.

'Well,' said Lidwell, 'Grant called at my house and told a different story. He told me he had met a few 'English Tommies' on the avenue. He gave me what he had taken, so here's the money, gold, watches and guns he took from ye. And here are the two guns he used to hold ye up,' and Lidwell placed the two cabbage stalks before the officers.

The next day those officers left the area, and it's said they were never seen in Ireland again.

Danes in Roscrea

When a princess of the O'Meara clan married a Limerick Dane her family were not happy with the marriage, but in the end it saved the people of Roscrea.

The young woman was often in the presence of her husband and his people when they discussed their business. Often they almost forgot she was there and that she was not one of them. And so it happened one day that she overheard them planning to attack and ravage the town of Roscrea. She sent a messenger to tell her family and warn the O'Meara clan of the danger. The O'Meara clan heeded her warning and got their men together to be ready.

On 29 July AD 845 there was a great fair in Roscrea, these fairs were famous and people came from not only all over Ireland but from other countries as well. Roscrea was full of buyers and sellers, farmers and merchants, Irish men and foreigners. In the midst of all these the Danes launched their attack, but the O'Mearas were ready, their men were ready and the farmers, merchants and foreigners of the fair. They drove the Danes back until they gave up on the attack. Roscrea was saved.

The Sacred Heart Sisters Roscrea

The Sacred Heart Sisters were founded in France in 1800. In 1842 the set up their first convent in Ireland, at Roscrea. The sisters have been a part of the education and history of Roascrea from then until 2014, when the remaining sisters moved to the house in Dublin and they left Roscrea for the last time. There are sure to be many stories of the work of the sisters over the 167 years they were there, this one is from famine times.

The Sacred Heart Sisters had a barrel by the front door in which they kept food parcels made up to give to any poor person who might knock, looking for charity. The parcels contained bread and meat and various vegetables. In the beginning, in the early 1840s, when the sisters first came to Roscrea very few people called, but by the end of that decade it was a different story. Famine had hit Ireland and the people of Tipperary suffered badly. Soon there was a steady stream of people looking for food and help in those difficult times. The sisters found it difficult to keep enough food to hand out; sometimes they were hard pressed to have enough food to feed themselves even.

One day two women called, asking for help. The sister who answered knew that there was only two loaves of bread left, and that had to feed the sisters in the convent as well. But the

two women begged and begged; they had families, children who were crying with the hunger, they said. When the sister heard this her heart was moved and she asked the two women to wait for a moment. She went to the Reverend Mother to ask her advice on what she should do as there was not another bit of food in the convent. The Reverend Mother listened to the story and told the sister to divide the last two loaves of bread between the two women. They might be in much more need of it than the sisters were and not to fear, God would provide. The sister obeyed and did as the Reverend Mother had said, giving out the last two loaves of bread to the two hungry women, who took them gratefully.

Shortly after this another knock came on the convent door, the sister answered and there was another mother asking for help and food to feed her family. 'I'm sorry m'am,' said the sister, 'We have no food left, look in the barrel.' They did, but when the sister looked in the barrel to her surprise she found it full to the brim with food. She was able to give that caller a parcel of food, and many other callers beside. It is said that that barrel did not run out for the whole duration of the famine. The sisters have continued to give help to those who knocked on their door, but in more recent times it hasn't been from the miraculous barrel.

Stories from the Famine

There were some counties who managed to escape the famine, and weren't hit to badly. Some had good landlords who nearly went broke trying to care for their tenants and the poor, but others had absentee landlords, and landlords who had no care or felt no responsibility for their people at all. Tipperary was one of the counties particularly affected by the famine.

There was a woman during the famine who had many children. She was getting desperate to find food and her children were always asking her for something to eat. One day in desperation and more to delay their disappointment, the mother began to boil a pot of stones. The stones were about the size of potatoes, and she had taken them and washed them and scrubbed them, just as she would do with potatoes, and put them in the pot to boil them. When the pot was boiled the children gathered around for their meal. The poor mother looked in their hungry little faces and not being able to delay their disappointment any longer she took the lid off the pot. To her surprise the pot was full of boiled potatoes and she and her family ate well that night.

Other people took more practical means to find food. One of the greatest disgraces of the famine was that there was plenty of food being grown, but the landlords sold it elsewhere. Only the potatoes were affected by the blight; turnips, carrots and wheat all grew strong and healthy. Some hungry people broke into the farmer's field to steal the crops and feed their families.

During black '47 there was a local landlord who had planted a field of turnips. With the shortage of food many of the locals had begun stealing the turnips, they would sneak into his field in the middle of the night and pull up the turnips when no one was looking. To stop this the landlord had two huts build in the field, one at either end, and into these he put an agent whose job it was to watch the field and run off any person trying to steal the turnips. But the watchmen employed had not the heart to run off the hungry people. They waited until the people had picked the turnips before they chased them away and they were never able to 'catch' anyone.

Others tried to let the little food they had last as long as it could, often doing without so that their families could eat. In Gurtnagoona, James Carroll told the story which he heard from his father. During the famine there was a family living off Indian meal. One day at breakfast the father ate nothing, saying he would leave his portion until later in the day. He went out to work in the garden but he died that morning, dropping dead from starvation. Another story he heard told of a man who had to turn his sow and *bonamhs* (piglets) loose because he could no longer afford to feed them. Another man took them in and looked after them and got paid for them after.

Sources

Abduction of Eleanor Arbuthnot: local websites and newspapers

Patrick Townsend: Source NFC 1119, p.282, from Patrick Commins, age 78

Jerrie Grant: NFC 547, pp.27–28 collected by Thomas Martin from his father Thomas Martin (Clonghisle)

Danes in Roscrea: NFC Schools 548, Scoil Lios Dubh, Dún Chiarán, Ikerrin, p.124, The Danes' Eileen ní Rian from Bean de Brún

The Sacred Heart Sisters Roscrea: NFC 548, pp.137–139 Brigid ní Treamfear collected from Mrs Sheedy, age 75

Stories from the Famine: NFC 547, pp.165–68 collected by James Carroll from his father, Clomemore School Killavinogue; NFC Schools 548, Scoil Lios Dubh, Dún Chiarán, Ikerrin, pp. 137–139 Eileen ní Rian from her grandfather Denis Ryan and Brigid ní Treamhear from Miss Shedy, age 75

10

The Battle of Widow McCormack's Cabbage Patch

The year 1848 was known as the year of the barricades. All over Europe ideas were changing; new ideals like liberty, equality and brotherhood were spoken about. The mood was caught in some of the literature of the time, like Victor Hugo's *Les Miserables*. Ireland too was caught in the wave of change. Fifty years after 1798, the United Irishmen might have gone but they were replaced by the Young Irelanders with names like Smyth O'Brien, Dillon and Davis to the fore.

The Young Irelanders were strongest in Tipperary, and Tipperary is where the only real battle of the movement took place. Tipperary lies in the Golden Vale, an area of rich agricultural land. The landowners here had amalgamated some of the farms and cleared the land of some of the tenants; whole villages had been swept away. The peasants had been retaliating since the 1700s, forming bands, 'whiteboys', groups of young men sworn to secrecy whose deeds could be just as bad as the landlords they stood against in the violence and vandalism they caused. From time to time there were rebellions and standoffs.

Of all the rebellions I learnt of in school, 1848 best caught my imagination, specifically 'The Battle of Widow McCormack's Cabbage Patch'.

Mr McCormack had the resources to build a stone, slate-roofed house. Jo O'Brien was the contractor who built the fine

house in 1844, the only one of its like in the neighbourhood. Mr McCormack had married a Houlihan from Callan, but died just year after the house was built, leaving Mrs McCormack a widow with five children. They continued to live in the house. On the day in question Mrs McCormack had left the children at home and gone into Ballingarry to hear William Smyth O'Brien speak about the Young Irelanders and their ideas.

Smyth O'Brien, Thomas Francis Meagher and John Blake Dillon were moving through south Leinster and Munster, gathering support to their cause. The RIC constables knew this and were not going to sit back and wait for the revolt to begin.

There had already been trouble in 1841 when a group of tenants had barricaded the roads to prevent a group from reaching Clonmel to cast their vote in the local election. This group of about forty-one men had left Cashel early in the morning, and stopped in Kilcoaly Abbey, the home of one of the candidates – Mr Baker – before continuing their journey. However, when they went to continue the journey they found the way barricaded at New Birmingham. A number of the local people had brought several cars full of coal and put them across the road, the people were armed with stones. When the men had emerged from their carriages to move the barricades the people attacked with stones, the police fired and general fighting broke out. There were a couple of people injured, including one man who lost an eye. The carriages were overturned, smashed and burned. The incident left the tenants and farmers having more faith in their own power and the landlords terrified.

The RIC could see that the Young Irelanders were attempting to amass a force together and so the RIC decided to move quickly on the leaders before they got too powerful.

On 29 July 1848 police from Killenaule, Callan, Thurles, Cashel and Kilkenny were under orders to converge on Ballingarry in the afternoon. Inspector Trent, with his white charger and sixty men, arrived around 10 a.m., much earlier than ordered. Smyth O'Brien and the Young Irelanders had been meeting on the roadside and when they heard that the soldiers were approaching they barricaded the road. Seeing the barricade, Trent turned his men in another direction. The Young Irelanders tried to head him off and Trent headed for the safest place he could find, somewhere that wouldn't catch fire too easily, that was solidly built and might withstand an attack and offer support and shelter to his men. Where else could he go but the best built house in the area – the house of Widow McCormack.

Some say that Trent was in such a hurry to reach the safety of the house that he left his pistol in the saddle bag of his horse. Trent and his soldiers rushed into the house and, locking the five children under the stairs, barricaded the house and settled themselves in for whatever was to come

Mrs McCormack was at the Young Irelander's rally listening to Smyth O'Brien addressing the people. When word was brought to her that the RIC had taken over her home with her children inside, she rushed home calling out that Smyth O'Brien had put her children in danger.

With Smyth O'Brien following close behind, eager to find a peaceful solution to releasing the children, Mrs McCormack approached the kitchen window of the house to speak with Trent. A crowd gathered around the house and its garden, many of them Young Irelander supporters. This was the first time the new flag that Smith O'Brien and Meagher had brought back from France, a tricolour, was unfurled; one stripe was orange – representing the Protestants of Ireland of which Smith O'Brien was one, one stripe was green – representing the Catholics of Ireland, and the stripe in the middle was white – representing a hope of peace between all. The flag is familiar now as our national flag, but its first unfurling was by Widow McCormack's cabbage patch in 1848.

Some of the unarmed crowd threw stones at the RIC constables in the house. The stones broke the window and the already nervous officers opened fire. Those of the rebels who had guns returned fire. Terence McManus pulled Smyth O'Brien out of the line of the fire, away through the wicket gate into the cabbage patch, John Walsh who had a gun was shot and the son of a local widow who was only spectating was killed. Some people tried to set fire to the house or smoke the police out, by putting damp straw by the door to burn.

The local priest, Fr Philip Fitzgerald, arrived to minister to the sick and dying. The head constable from Kilkenny, Constable O'Carroll, arrived in plain clothes with a white flag and he and Fr Fitzgerald approached the Young Irelander leaders and got them to

disperse the crowd. At the same time reinforcements were arriving from Cashel, led by Inspector Cox. The rebel leaders, knowing what might be in store if they were caught, fled.

McManus and Meagher were captured by 12 August; Smyth O'Brien managed to stay at large until 9 October. Terence McManus had borrowed a horse from a friend. He later sent the horse back again and the friend was brought to give evidence at the trial. One story tells how the friend was asked to point out the person who had taken his horse. The friend looked around the court and then pointed at the judge and said, 'There's the man who took my horse.' McManus himself is quoted as saying at the trial 'it's not that I loved England less, just that I loved Ireland more'. McManus was sent to Van Diemen's Land from which he escaped in 1852.

William Smyth O'Brien went on the run; he got to Thurles where he spent a night in a friend's house. The next day, seeing the English soldiers were nearby, he left his gun with his friend and continued on. Passing through Thurles he saw a notice offering a £500 reward for information which would lead to his arrest. He saw an old woman nearby, whose struggle to make ends meet could be seen and approached her, 'I'm William Smyth O'Brien,' he said to her, 'If you turn me in you can make £500 for yourself.'

'Well,' she answered, 'that money will be a long time unclaimed if they're waiting on me to give information. My honour is dearer to me than money.' Shortly after that O'Brien was captured and brought to trial. He too was sentenced to transportation to Van Diemans Land, but later was pardoned and returned to Ireland to live a quiet life.

Mrs McCormack and her five children emigrated to the US in 1855. The house in Balingarry is now the 'War House' museum.

Sources
NFC 1119, p.258 from John Morris, age 77, from Killenaule; Revd Philip Fitzgerald notes from narrative of proceedings against confederates, *Nenagh Guardian*, 21 July 1841, p.4

11

HUNTED PRIESTS AND HIDDEN TREASURE

Laws restricting Catholic involvement in political and social life had been creeping into English rule from the time of Elizabeth I. Towards the end of the 1600s they were at their worst. Not only Catholics were affected; the laws affected Presbyterians and Quakers as well, but in Ireland it was the Catholic poor who most felt the force of the laws. The laws banned intermarriage, did not recognise Presbyterian marriages, and excluded Catholics and Presbyterians from many positions of employment, especially positions of power and influence.

Everyone had to pay a tithe to the Established Church (Church of England). Catholics were barred from carrying arms, entering politics, voting, being on a jury, teaching, inheriting property or owning a horse. Priests had to register themselves and stay within their registered district. Any priest not registered by 1705 was to be removed from the country and, if found preaching, charged with treason.

Anyone found in breach of the laws, either a Catholic or those helping Catholics, could be penalised. Punishment was not uniform across the country; it very much depended on the local magistrates, and so there were pockets where Catholic and Protestant got on side by side well enough, but there were other places where the animosity was very much felt. Up to the 1780s the priests had a pretty hard time of it.

In the 1640s Cromwell's men seemed to make a point of upholding the laws; they desecrated many of the churches, abbeys and monasteries across the country. They took whatever treasures they could find, murdered many monks and sent the priests running and hiding, fearing for their lives. Across the county there are stories of treasures hidden to keep them from the Cromwellians, and tales of priests in hiding, often helped by sympathising Protestants. Lots of these stories are to be found in the National Folklore Collection in UCD, particularly in the School's Collection, maybe because for the children there is a fascination in finding hidden treasure. These are just some of the stories and don't be surprised to find that there may be a field near you where it is reputed treasure was buried or someone was hidden. Not all of them refer to Cromwellian times but they all have a mention of either 'treasure' or 'priests'.

ROSCREA

At the Church of St Crónán in Roscrea there is a large cross with the carving of a figure. It is believed that the figure is that of St Crónán himself and that the cross marks the place where the saint is buried. When Cromwell's soldiers came they tried to desecrate the cross. They began with the knees of the saintly figure and tried to cut them or chisel them out, but when they did, blood poured from the cross and the soldiers fell dead. The knees of the figures on the cross separated from the rest of the body then, and can be seen further down on the cross. The monks in Roscrea were in fear of their lives and needed a means to escape.

Now, there was a secret passage between the church in Roscrea and Monahincha, where St Crónán's original settlement had been, and a tower at Monanhinch where the monks could hide and, once the ladder was drawn up, be safe from the Cromwellians. The monks made their escape down the tunnel, leaving the soldiers searching for them. The soldiers couldn't find the passage, though they suspected that there was one. So they offered money to anyone who would give them the information they required.

One woman came forward to take the money, and she revealed where the entrance to the tunnel was but, as she did, she turned to stone there and then, as she was, with a basket on her head and all. There is a figure of stone outside of Monahincha church said to be her.

The monks got to the tower and climbed up the ladder. Had they pulled up the ladder behind them then this might have been a very different story, but they forgot and the soldiers followed them up into the tower and killed them all.

Other soldiers had come up from Tenderry in tin boats. They chased and executed any monks they caught, hanging them from the trees around Monahincha. These trees were later sold to people in the locality for fire wood but they would not burn.

The monks had thrown all their valuables, bibles, vessels, candlesticks etc, into the lake in Monahincha as they tried to flee from the soldiers. The treasures lay at the bottom of the lake for a long time. Later the land came into the possession of Birches of Birch Grove. Mr Birch hired a diver to find the treasure in the lake. The diver came up with a gold candlestick. Birch and the diver examined the candlestick and the diver turned to Birch, 'I'll help draw up the treasure for half of what you find in the lake,' he said.

'No,' said Birch, 'Is not my money good enough without my having to give you half?' so the diver threw the candlestick back into the lake.

Birch hired several men to drain the lake. The men tried but the water would not go. Birch took up a shovel and struck the water in the devil's name, the water went roaring along, but the hand Birch had held the shovel in was sore for a long time. It festered and would not heal. Birch got worse and died. He was buried in Monahincha in the Catholic graveyard there, even though he was Protestant, because he was fond of the place. It was the same graveyard where the murdered monks would have been buried. As he was dying Birch is said to have said that he thought very bad of leaving. The clergyman with him said, 'Don't you know you'll be going to a better place?' Birch's reply was 'By God I doubt it.'

PAUL HIGGINS

Paul Higgins was a Protestant rector in Templemore, he died in 1724 when it was still a crime to be Catholic and Catholic priests could be arrested and hanged. The story was that Paul Higgins had been a Catholic priest and had changed religion to save his life, avoid persecution and to be able to marry. There was a story that one time when Paul was ministering to his flock from the pulpit in Templemore church, there was a terrible thunder storm. The thunder was fierce loud and the lightening frightening, and the storm was right over the church. Paul is said to have stopped his sermon, blessed himself, and called out to his parishioners, 'Bless yerselves, ye divils or ye'll all be damned!'

It seems that Paul never forgot his Catholic roots though, and the story is that he kept his friendship with some of the priests he had studied with. He had an understanding with one friend that when it came to his death this friend would come to give him his Last Rights. Well, in 1724 that day came for Paul as it will for all of us. He sent word to his priest friend that he was dying and the friend arrived to see Paul. When they were behind closed doors, Paul made his confession, reconciled himself to the Church and was given the Last Rights. His friend stayed with him right up to the end, and when he died, the friend laid him out in his priestly vestments on his death bed.

Leaving the house the priest friend told the servants that Paul was resting and not to disturb him for a couple of hours. He then got as far away from the house as he could before the body was discovered and the priest hunters sent after him. When the servants did eventually look in on Paul there was a mighty to-do about him being in priestly vestments on the death bed, but it was too late for him to suffer any persecution because of it.

SCART'S BANK

In the 1650s there were no banks and many people hid their money in the ground. It was said that there was money hidden in a field owned by Mr Stanley in Scart. The story was that the money was hidden near a stone where a small bush was growing.

One night in 1659 Meagher went to dig and look for this money, but he pricked his finger and hurt it and so couldn't continue digging and had to go home. A day or two later, three men came to dig as well, but the ground was too hard and despite their iron tools they couldn't get through it and so they went home. One of that three found later that he had left his tool behind him so he returned in the morning to get it. But when he returned he found the soil soft and easy to dig. They took it as a sign and no one ever tried to dig for the money again.

COLD SHOULDER

During the Penal Times there was a landlord who was evicting a tenant. He was a descendant of the Cromwellian planter Vaughan and it was an old woman he was evicting. The local priest petitioned on behalf of the old woman, asking Vaughan not to evict her. But the landlord refused. The priest put his hand on Vaughan's shoulder and told him that something else would bother him before his death which would be soon. A couple of weeks later, Vaughan died trying to eat the shoulder where the priest had touched him.

A HUNTING PRIEST

Not all the stories about priests involve them being hunted and having to hide. Some were even about priests who liked to hunt, as this one did. This was collected from Billy Treacy by pupils from Clonmore School.

A local priest by the name of Fr Doyle liked hunting. He was hunting one day in Longfordwood on the land where St Crónán's School is now built. The land was part of the Mount Frisco Estate, land owned by the Lloyds. Father Doyle had two greyhounds with him and was caught by the gameskeeper, a man named Fogarty. Fogarty brought Fr Doyle to court and he was fined €10 for hunting illegally, within an hour of news of the fine the parishioners had got together and gathered the money to pay the priest's fine. Father Doyle turned to Fogarty and said to him, 'A time will come when there will be more rabbits and hares than sheep or cattle in Mount Frisco, no one in the big house will ever have any luck and a day will come when jackdaws will fly in and out through the broken windows.'

Strange to say, such is the case today.

GOLDEN GROVE

There was a priest in Penal Times who received a message to go to Golden Grove where a man was very ill and dying and calling for him. The priest went to answer the call. When he arrived at the house he asked to see the man, but was told he was much better now and didn't need a priest. The priest said he would see him anyway.

When he was coming back down from the room there were soldiers waiting for him; the man had not been sick at all but laying a trap to catch the priest. But a girl from the Vaughan family took the priest out of the house another way, and out of Golden Grove to safety. Soon after that the man who had pretended to be ill really did get sick and died.

THE LADY OF CLONAN

A lady in Clonan also hid her treasure in Cromwellian times. A week after she died, a man came to dig looking for the money, he dug a little here and there, when suddenly the ghost of the lady appeared to him. He was so frightened that he fell unconcious. When he awoke the soil he had disturbed in his digging had been put back and looked as if it had never been touched. The man got the message, went home and never returned.

From then on the ghost of the lady was known to appear from time to time at that spot. A local priest came to hear of this and he went one time to the place to try persuade the ghost of the lady to leave. The Lady of Clonan laid her ghostly hands on the face of the priest leaving the marks of her fingers on his face.

She prophesied that no one would find her treasure, not until they had a black cock with one white feather. She left after that due to the power of the priest and has not been seen since. The treasure could still be there today.

HIDDEN TREASURE IN MRS MURRAY'S FIELD

There was a story around Dun Chairan that there was treasure buried in Mrs Murray's field. Some of the inhabitants remembered being told stories by their grandfathers about their attempt to get the treasure in the 1830s.

Two brothers, John and Pat Leahy, and their uncle, Michael Quinlan, dreamt for three consecutive nights that there was gold in the field. The dream was very vivid and the instructions very clear. The gold was to be dug up at night in absolute silence, the light they used was to be quenched three times and he who relit it would lose the sight of one eye.

So the three men got ready to collect their treasure. They would carry out the operation on a calm evening and wait until late, when everyone would be in bed. On the chosen night the three of them set off around midnight to the spot in Lisduff and began to dig in silence.

Unknown to them not everyone was in bed. There was a card night in Bigg's house not far from the spot, and all were wide

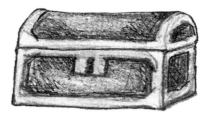

awake. Biggs and his guests heard the noise of spades and shovels. They set out to find out what was going on, and, just in case, Mr Bigg brought his gun with him.

When they arrived at the spot where the men were digging, Biggs asked what was going on but of course he got no answer as the men had to work in silence. Biggs fired shots over their heads and the light went out. John Leahy relit the light and immediately he lost the sight in one of his eyes. That put an end to the treasure hunt once and for all. That pot of gold might be still in Mrs Murray's field though she herself is long, long dead and gone.

O'MEAGHER'S FORT TREASURE

It is said that in the 1600s, the O'Meaghers also buried their treasure in the ground near their fort. They left one of their daughters to guard it and the story is that Cromwell's soldiers came along and asked the young girl what she was doing. She did not answer them or give them a satisfactory answer so at midnight they beheaded her. Her ghost is said to still guard the buried treasure belong to the O'Meaghers.

THE WHEEL

On land owned by the O'Mearas of Ballyuckard there is a fort or *rath* to be seen and on the outside a large rock. Two neighbouring men dreamt on three consecutive nights that there was hidden gold buried on one side of the fort, near the rock. The dream was very vivid and in it they both saw that as they dug down they would firstly come across the stock of wheel, and further down the lid of a baker and lastly a flag before they would uncover the gold.

On the fourth day the two men set out, prepared with shovels and spades, to verify the dream. They went to the spot of the dream and began to dig. As in the dream they soon came across the stock of the wheel, they removed it and continued digging. A little further down they came across the lid of the baker and took that out. Just a little deeper they came to the flag. The two men tried to remove the flag but each time they thought they had, it fell back down on top of them. After a time the two men gave up and went back home. They each found themselves confined to bed for the next three weeks, suffering from pains and unable to move.

An Old Miser

There was a woman who lived alone. She was old and sick. Her neighbours, who were not terribly well-off, used to call to her to make tea and see that she was alright. It was clear now though that she was failing and would soon die and so the neighbours did all they could to comfort her and make her comfortable. The old woman would give instructions from time to time as to how she would like her funeral, she picked out the clothes in which she was to be laid out for her wake, but gave instructions that her hair was not to be touched.

When she died the neighbouring women did all they could to follow her instructions. They laid her out as she had asked, dressed her in the clothes she had picked and left her hair alone. The woman must have had a head of long thick hair, because she had it caught up in a great big bun at the back of her head.

Just before the funeral the coffin arrived and the undertakers lifted the body and put it into the coffin, but here was the problem: the bun on the back of the woman's head was so big that it lifted the woman's head out of the coffin when she was lying straight. Unless they were to turn the woman's head to the side they couldn't put the lid on the coffin.

The women turned to each other.

'If we loosened the bun on the back of her head we could lower her the fraction that would be needed to put the lid on the coffin.

'But she specifically asked that her hair not be touched.'

'What harm can it do to loosen it just a little? She can lie respectable in the coffin.'

So the women decided to loosen the bun. When they did, they were surprised to find that the woman's hair was full of small rolls of paper. She had all her money rolled up and hidden in her hair. The women went to the priest and told him what had happened. They themselves were loath to touch the money as the woman was so particular about not touching her hair and obviously preferred that it go to the grave with her than do good for anyone else. The priest too wanted nothing to do with the money. In the end it was given to the relieving officer and I hope he got to do some good with it.

Scath na Legaune

Dick Cassidy lived not far from Holy Cross Abbey in a farm house. Each year he made a place for John Curtain who arrived looking for work. John was a good worker and had proved himself to Dick, but more than that he was a good storyteller and singer and while there was work enough to keep him in employment, Dick enjoyed the evenings in John's company, listening to his stories and songs.

One night while John was staying with Mr Cassidy he had a strange dream. He dreamt that an old man dressed in clothes of old Ireland came to him and said, 'John Curtain do you know where you are?'

'I do,' answered John, 'I'm in Dick Cassidy's house.'

'This land once belonged to your family long ago,' said the old man.

'It's a pity then that we lost it,' said John, 'It would have been nice to have owned this land.'

'There are treasures of our family still buried on this land, which will make you and fifty like you rich beyond measure, if you'll listen to me,' said the old man, and he continued, 'Do you know the height above the abbey, the blessed spot where the piece of the blessed cross fell from its hiding place at the sweet sound of the bells, and the good woman met her son after he travelling to Jerusalem to get it. And do you know the old bush there, '*Scath na Legaune*', by the road on a little bank of earth and stones. You must dig on the line between that bush and the tower of the abbey, 6ft from the bush in the dead of night and in complete silence, and you will find the treasure.'

John woke the next morning and thought little of the dream, only that it had been interesting. But that night he had the same dream again, with the same old man and the same message. The following day he took a walk up towards the bush and looked at it. That third night he had the same dream again, although this time the old man seemed a little angry that John had taken no action yet. When John woke in the morning he felt there must be something in the dream if he had had the same dream three nights in a row. He decided to talk to Dick about his strange dream and see what he thought.

Dick was a man who believed in the power of dreams and, when he heard that John had had the same dream three nights in a row, agreed that they should go and dig in the spot the old man had pointed out. That night, after a good supper and a sup of whiskey to keep them warm, the two men headed off near midnight with shovels and picks. They made their way to the bush near the side of the road, growing on the bank of stones and earth. They measured 6ft on the line between that bush and the tower of the abbey and they began to dig. They worked away in silence. After about an hour digging Dick's shovel hit off something. He signalled to John who joined him in the hole and the two men cleared away the loose clay and dirt. They found a flagstone, but it was so big and heavy that the two men couldn't possibly lift it themselves. Dick covered up the flagstone again and headed home, explaining that he thought they should return the following night when they would bring other men to help.

The following day Dick called together a couple of men to help in the work, promising each of them a share in whatever would be found underneath the flagstone. But the three men were unsure about following instructions from a dream. Dick talked and argued and cajoled them; he gave the each a dram of whiskey and they began to soften. After a feed of supper and a few more drams of whiskey the men agreed to go with Dick and John and dig up the treasure.

Dick explained to them how important it was to remain absolutely silent while the work was ongoing or else they would lose all hope of the treasure. Just before midnight the five men headed off together with shovels and crowbars, back to the spot near the old bush on the line between it and the tower of Holy Cross Abbey. In silence they worked, they uncovered the flagstone and then, with many gestures, grimaces and hand signals, they levered the stone up and over. Under that flagstone there was a staircase going deep underground.

Dick had a candle with him which he lit and led the way down the staircase. All four men followed him, John first, then the other three. At the bottom of the stairs was a long passage. At the end of the passage was a door, partly open and through that door another door, closed but with a grate on it. The men walked on in silence and gathered around the closed door. Dick held up the candle and one of the men looked through the grate, 'Hurrah, me boys,' said he, 'By Noonan's ghost we are all made men.' The words had hardly passed his lips when there was a terrible crashing noise like the whole place was falling in. A wind blew out the candle, leaving the men in darkness. Quickly they fumbled and made their way back out the passage and up the staircase.

When they came out again into the night they looked back at the abbey and swore they could see flames dancing on top of the tower. Frightened, they quickly each made their ways home.

The next morning they met together and agreed that that night they should go again and try for the treasure, for the man who had looked through the door swore that it was a great treasure lay there and it would be pity to leave it. That night, just before midnight, they made their way in silence to the bush and to the place where the flagstone was. But lo, for all the digging Dick and John had done the place was now completely covered over and looked as though the ground had never been disturbed. It was covered in daisies and buttercups.

That night John had another dream. This time the old man appeared to him angry at him for not following the instructions.

'For all your learning you'd be better without it.' John had lost his chance to be rich; that treasure would be locked up for another hundred years, and as far as I know it's buried there still.

Sources

Roscrea: collected by Emily Carroll from her father for the 1937 schools collection; Nellie Prince collected from Ned Quinlan

Paul Higgins: NFC 548, Scoil Clochar na Trocaire, Teampall Mor, Eliogarty, pp.193–210, 'Paul Higgins' from Michael Carey, age 84

Scart's Bank: NFC 549, pp.5–7 collected by Madeling Monogue from John Maher, age 76, Roscrea

Cold Shoulder: NFC 548, Scoil Clochar na Trocaire, Teampall Mor, Eliogarty, p.158, collected by Eileen Ryan from her father Roddy Ryan

A Hunting Priest: NFC 548, Clonmore School, Killavinogue, Ikerrins, p.203, from Billy Treacy, age 63

Golden Grove: NFC 548, Scoil Clochar na Trocaire, Teampall Mor, Eliogarty, pp.160–161, 'Golden Grove' collected by Made McDonnell from her aunt Kate Delaney

The Lady of Clonan: NFC 549, Scoil an Clochar, Roscrea, Barony of Ikerrin, Tipperary, pp.40–42, collected by Maura Moore from John Maher, age 67

Hidden Treasure in Mrs Murray's Field: NFC 548, Scoil Lios Dubh, Dún Chiarán, Ikerrin, pp.8–11, 'Mrs Murray's Field' James Jones, Martin McCann 55, Ned Hegarty 35, Mick Gleeson 35

O Meagher's Fort Treasure: NFC 548, Sorcha ní Meachair, from Eamon O'Breathnach pp.118 & 129

The Wheel: NFC 548, Scoil Lios Dubh, Dún Chiarán, Ikerrin, p.122, 'Treasure Wheel' Mainín ne Meacair from Con Troy

An Old Miser: NFC 700, p.215, collected by Seosamh O'Dálaigh from Mary Hurley, age 81, Thurles, 1940

Scath na Legaune: *Fairy Legends and Traditions of South Ireland* by Thomas Crofton Croker (1825)

12

Fr Nicholas Sheehy

Father Nicholas Sheehy was born in 1728. He studied in Spain and became parish priest for Sanraheen, Ballysheehan and Templetenny. He could be quite outspoken about the wrongs he saw around him at the time: the treatment of tenants, the neglect of the poor. This made him popular among his people but not among the Protestant land-lords. He was told to take a pledge that he wouldn't say anything 'rebellious' but he wouldn't; whatever he had to say he'd say.

On one occasion, he was brought to court, charged with having been involved with the 'whiteboys' who had carried out some act of vandalism nearby, but after a fair trial Fr Sheehy was acquitted.

On that occasion the story is told locally that it was Judge Gore who presided over that hearing and on his journey home the 'white-boys' stopped his carriage. They unhitched his horses from under the carriage and began to draw the carriage themselves. Judge Gore was terrified; the 'whiteboys' had been responsible for many terrible deeds, and how was he to know that these actions were a way of honouring him and showing how much his honesty and integrity were appreciated in a time when the reverse was presumed.

However, not all the judges were like Judge Gore. There was another time when a local man went missing, this man had been an informer on the 'whiteboys', he had every reason to go missing as the authorities were pressing him to inform, and who knows

what the 'whiteboys' would do to him if they caught him. Whether
he was dead or in hiding no one knew but Fr Sheehy was charged
with his murder in 1764. He went into hiding.

For a while he stayed hidden, people around sheltering him,
but he saw that there was a reward on his head so he couldn't keep
hiding but he knew he wouldn't get a fair trial in Clonmel. He wrote
to the authorities in Dublin, stating he would give himself up if,
and only if, he could be tried in Dublin. They agreed and Fr Sheehy
was brought to Dublin to await trial. He was treated very well there;
it seemed obvious he was not guilty. Can you be tried for murder
when there is no proof of a crime, no body, no witnesses? Father
Sheehy was there nearly nine months before his trial took place.

At the trial no mention was made of the supposed murder. Fr
Sheehy was charged with treason (in being a practising Catholic)
and was found not guilty. Everyone cheered in the court, pleased
he would be released. But no, just as it all seemed to be clear the
judge said that there was another matter which needed to be sorted
out, and that was that Fr Nicholas Sheehy was accused of being
party to the deliberate and wilful murder of John Bridges.

'Well I can't say as I'm surprised,' said Fr Sheehy, 'Given those
who have brought the charges against me, but I must say, if it is a
case that Mr Bridges has been murdered, and God forbid that he
has, I had no part or knowledge of the deed.'

Father Sheehy was transported to Clonmel to face trial, and he
received none of the comforts nor respect on that journey that he
had in Dublin. The trial came to pass but none of the local bar-
risters would represent him; they were too frightened. In the end it
was a young barrister from Dublin who represented him in court.

The witnesses were called. One was Moll Dunlea, a woman
whose choice of lifestyle brought her no good words from the
priest. Some said it was because Fr Sheehy had put her out of the
church one time, now, to get back at him, she said that she had
overheard the plan for the murder and had followed the men who
carried it out. Moll's mother said that Moll slept in the same bed as

her every night and that there was no way she could have left the house on the night of the murder without her knowing.

Another witness was a man called Touhy, a horse thief, who swore he had seen Fr Sheehy with a group of 'whiteboys' planning the murder, and afterwards taking the body of John Bridges to bury it. He had to be let out of prison to testify. Others were to testify on Fr Sheehy's behalf, but some were so intimidated by the prosecution that their words were fumbled or they withdrew. In the end, the jury decided he was guilty and should be hung, drawn and quartered. Father Sheehy spoke at the end, saying that the event was a gross injustice, and the result of perjury but that he left it in God's hands to decide between the guilty and the innocent. He was carted away to prison to await his execution.

They say that while Fr Sheehy was waiting to be hanged, the doors of the prison opened and he could have gone free, but he didn't; he let one of the other men go instead. All the time he kept cool and calm, even in the face of death.

On the 15 March 1766 Fr Nicholas Sheehy was hanged, drawn and quartered. His head was placed on a spike outside Clonmel prison for all to see. After twenty years on the spike, a blizzard came which no living human could stand and the skull was blown down. Mrs Catherine Burke, his sister, retrieved it and buried it with the rest of his body in Sahraheen.

Later someone ran into Mr Bridge in Newfoundland where he had emigrated to. He was told that Fr Sheehy had been hanged for his murder. Bridges was in shock; he had no idea that the priest had been hanged for him.

There is a beautiful stained-glass window in memory of Fr Sheehy in Sanraheen today.

Sources
NFC 700, pp.46–47 and 199 from Joe Fannin, age 79, Two-Mile-Borris, collected by Seosamh O'Dalaigh; www.bcparish.com wikepedia; *My Clonmel Scrapbook*

13

FAIRYTALES AND LORE

There is a rich tradition around the fairies in Tipperary, as there is in many other counties of Ireland. Areas of natural beauty such as the Glen of Aherlow invite the belief of a magical life behind the ordinary.

THE BLACKSMITH

Fogarty, the blacksmith, and his wife and son, lived at Bansha on the Cahir Road. One late November's night there was a loud knock at the forge door. Fogarty got up to answer the knock. It was the rule of the road at that time for a smith to put up a shoe *gratis* for any traveller who might pass if his horse had lost one.

Well, when he opened the door he found a tall dark man standing outside holding a sloe-black horse.

'Shoe my horse, smith,' said the stranger.

'All right,' said the smith.

There and then he went to work; he rose a heat and welded a shoe. He then lifted the horse's hoof he stripped off the old slipper, and put on the new shoe. When the job was finished the man and the horse left the forge, the man remarking that the smith would find himself paid in the morning. Next morning the smith found a gold shoe on the floor instead of the slipper he had taken off the night before. He told no one but his wife of the find and they had the golden shoe melted down.

The same time the next year the stranger called again, again demanding that his horse be shod. As before the smith went to work; he rose a fire to make the shoe, removed the slipper and put the new shoe in place, and as before the smith woke in the morning to find a golden horse shoe in place of the slipper he had removed the night before. For several years this continued. Once a year the smith awakened by the stranger in the middle of the night to shoe his horse and in the morning the smith finding a golden shoe.

But the smith's wife was uneasy as to where the golden shoes were coming from. She felt the money couldn't have been 'got right' and urged her husband to see a priest. The smith did so, and told the priest the story of the stranger and the golden shoes. The priest asked him to wait a fortnight till he could find out more information, and so then help him.

As the time for the yearly visit grew close again, the smith went back to visit the priest. This time the priest had an answer for him.

'Work away as usual,' said the priest, 'But as you are putting the shoe on the horse take a look at the hind hooves, if they are cloven ask the rider 'Is it the North or South that won?'

When the stranger arrived again, the smith went on with his work as usual. The stranger wanted one of the foremost shoes done, and as the smith was putting the shoe on the horse's hoof he glanced back at the hind hooves. Sure enough, they were cloven.

'Was it the North or South that won sir?' asked the smith

The stranger was startled and answered savagely, 'It was the North won the last two consecutive years and damn your informant.'

Before the smith recovered from the shock the stranger was in his saddle and gone, the next morning the old slipper of the horse was still where it had been dropped on the floor, there was no golden shoe and the stranger never called again.

'Did the Tailor get the Thread Yet?'

Down at Bearna there once lived a farmer named Dwyer. This was during the time when the tailors would work in the farmer's houses, and the farmer's wives used to card and spin the wool from their own sheep. The weavers of Tipperary would weave it into fine cloth which was then ready for whenever the tailor would come. The tailors were busy in those days, and guaranteed work, and often a farmer and his family might be waiting for the tailor long after he had promised to come.

This particular tailor had come to Bearna to Dywer's and was working away mighty. He had promised to be in the next town the following week and had young Dwyer's suit to finish first. The tailors often preferred to work on the kitchen table as there was more light in the kitchen and a good surface to work on. On the Saturday evening the tailor came off the table.

'Your suit is nearly finished,' he said, 'I know you were anxious to have it for Sunday, for tomorrow but I have no more thread left to sew on the buttons.'

'Hold on there a minute,' said the young man, 'Oola is not so very far away. I can be there and back before you know it and I'll bring plenty of thread for you to sew on the buttons.' And he picked up his stick and left for Oola there and then.

Night came but the young man had not returned. His family were worried and they called some neighbours and together they searched the road to Oola, along with the shortcut. Come day-break they found the young man's body alongside a double ditch on the way to Oola. They took home the corpse, waked him and buried him.

A year later when all the family were sitting eating super the door opened and in walked that same young man. Many at the table screamed and fled. Just his father remained.

'Father,' asked the young man, 'Did the tailor get the thread yet?'

'Yerra,' said the father, 'that's more than twelve months ago since your tailor was here. Didn't we wake you and bury you since that, and what's troubling you now to bring you back?'

The young man was shocked, he told his father that as he travelled to Oola he had crossed the double ditch and came across a hurling game. Two teams were playing and, being a good hurler himself, he stopped a while to watch the game. A man came up with a spare hurly and invited him to join in. Another man had come up at the same time, telling him not to mind the first but to continue on his way. But the young Dywer enjoyed playing hurling and for the sport he took up the hurly offered him and joined in the game.

Dwyer didn't think he could have been more than five minutes playing the game when it ended. He went into a nearby house with the other players to rest for a bit. The group of men then went filing out through the door but none of them invited him to join them so Dwyer stayed where he was.

When all the men had gone, a very old man came over to him and said 'If you want to go home I can let you off now if you like.'

He was happy for someone to show him the way home, for the place was strange to him, the men strange, and even the house had seemed strange to him.

When he came to himself again he found himself on the Hill of Derk. As he was nearing home he remembered his message but was aware something had come over him and decided to continue home first.

He made it clear to his father all he knew of where he had been, all his friends and neighbours came to see him after him coming back. But the mystery remained – how the body they buried could be of the same man as him that came back to live for years after in Bearna.

Sources
The Blacksmith: *Bealoideas*, Iml 4 Uimhir 3 (1934), pp.278–9 collected by Martin Burke
'Did the Tailor get the Thread Yet?': Bealoideas, Iml 4 Uimhir 3 (1934), pp.278–9 collected by Martin Burke from Thomas Power.

14

KNOCKSHEGOWNA

Knockshegowna is a townland in County Tipperary, not far from Ballingarry as you travel towards the Laois border. Its translation is *Cnoic Shí Gabhna*, 'Hill of the Fairy Calf'. Well, there has to be a story in that, and there is.

Close to the top of the hill at Knockshegowna there is a pasture area, a lovely place enticing to any herdsman to pasture his cattle or sheep. But that area had once been a fairy spot before human kind had come to live in the area.

Now, the fairies were getting fed up with the mournful sound of cattle lowing on one of their dancing grounds and they plotted as to how to rid the spot of the cattle, sheep and herdsmen. How better of course than to frighten away the men in such a manner so as they wouldn't return, and would spread the word to others not to venture near the spot either.

So in the night, once the cattle were settled and easy and the herdsmen wrapped in their cloaks, the fairy queen came and danced. As she danced, she changed her form from one hideous frightening being to another. First she was a horse with the wings of an eagle and the tail of a dragon, then a little man with a lame leg and a bull's head, then a great ape with duck's feet and a turkey tail. I could go on all day about the shapes she shifted herself into.

And she made noises, terrible frightening noises, hisses, howls, hoots, screams, neighs and cackles, as was never heard in this world before.

The poor herdsmen covered their faces and cried to all the saints of heaven for help but it was no use. A puff of the fairy woman's breath moved their cloak from their faces, and, try as they might, they could not look away for they were rooted to the spot for the duration of her dance. The hair of their necks rose and their teeth almost fell out from chattering; the cattle were driven into a mad frenzy from fear and the poor herdsman were rooted to the spot till dawn came and the sun rose over the hill.

The poor cattle were pining away from night after night of disturbed rest and there seemed no end to the accidents. Each night there was sure to be some accident or other, a cow falling into a pit, or into the river and getting maimed, hurt or even killed. And the herdsmen, well the farmer had gone through so many herdsmen by this time it was hard for him to find another, no one wanted to herd on Knockshegowna. The farmer offered double, then treble, then quadruple the money for the herding of his cattle, but not a man could be found who would go through the horror of facing the fairies.

The fairies rejoiced in the success of their efforts, and with the herd thinning and the herdsmen afraid to set foot on the land the fairies came back in numbers, gambolling and dancing on their green.

The farmer was greatly troubled for he had his bills to pay and a landlord who looked for rent. If he couldn't pasture his herd on the land what had he? Everyone he had asked had refused to bring the herd up to Knockshegowna. Who was left to ask?

One day while walking deep in thought the farmer met Larry Hoolihan. Larry was a piper and a good one at that, an equal to his piping was not known for fifteen parishes. With a few drinks inside him, Larry feared nothing; he would defy the devil himself, face a mad bull, even fight single handed against the whole fair. Larry met the farmer this day, saw he was troubled and asked him what was wrong. The farmer told Larry of his misfortunes.

'What am I to do Larry? No one will herd my cattle. How am I to fatten the cattle enough to get a decent price for them?'

'If that's all that ails you,' said Larry, 'worry no more. It would be a fine thing if I who was never afraid of any man should be afraid of a fairy no bigger than my thumb.'

'Mind what you say,' warned the farmer, 'You don't know who's listening, but if you can stay with my cattle for a week on the mountain you'll never want for anything again.' A bargain was struck and that evening as the moon was rising Larry took his place on Knockshegowna to watch over the cattle. As soon as he was settled on a comfortable rock out of the wind and cold, he took out his pipes and began to play.

It wasn't long till the fairies made their presence felt. He heard them laugh and one say, 'What, another man disturbing the peace of our fairy ring? Go show him Queen what happens to men who disturb our peace,' and with that Larry heard a rustling and felt a wind on his face and when he looked up he saw a great black cat poised above him, the cat leapt and became a salmon in a bow tie before him.

'Go on jewel,' said Larry, 'If you dance I'll play,' and he played his best and she turned first from this and into that and then from that into this, but it was not having the desired effect on the new herder. He just continued on playing, and meeting her movements in the rhythm and mood of his music. She decided to try a new tactic and changed into a new white calf, gentle and calm – or so it seemed. The calf fawned and lowed, great big brown eyes on her and moved closer to Larry hoping to catch him off guard but Larry was not to be fooled by the fairy's tricks. As soon as the calf was close enough he downed the pipes and leapt on her back.

Now as you look westward from the top of Knockshegowna you can see the River Shannon flowing 10 miles away. The fairy calf, seeing this as a great opportunity to better Larry, took a great leap and in one bound landed on the other side of the river. Larry fell from her back onto the soft turf, he looked up at the calf and, looking her in the eye, said, 'By my word! Well done. That was not a bad leap – for a calf.'

The fairy queen gave up, she resumed her own shape.

'You're a bold fellow Larry,' she said. 'Will you go back as you came?'

'I will,' said Larry, 'If you'll let me.' She turned into a calf again and Larry got on her back. In one bound he was back on the top of Knockshegowna again. The fairy queen took her own shape again and addressed Larry.

'You've shown much courage Larry,' said she, 'so much so that I promise that as long as you tend the herds here, we will not harm or disturb you. Go and tell the farmer this and if ever we can be of assistance to you, you need only ask.'

The fairies kept their word and for as long as Larry herded there on the top of the hill he was never harassed or bothered by them. He watched the herd on the hill and played his pipes and the farmer was true to his word. He had a room built for Larry in his house, fed him and clothed him and paid him well. Larry was a constant presence on Knockshegowna till his death, and he was buried in the valley of Tipperary. Whether the fairies returned to the hill after that or not I couldn't tell you – you might have to visit the hill top on a clear night to find out.

Sources
Fairy Legends and Traditions from the South of Ireland by Thomas Crofton Croker (1825)

15

KNOCKGRAFFON

Just a couple of miles outside of Cahir you come the townland of Knockgraffon. There you will clearly see the moat of Knockgraffon; you can't miss it, it stands as dominating over the landscape today as it did long ago. For centuries it has been a place of historical and sacred importance. *Cnoc Rath Fionn* (Knockgraffon), the hill of the rath of Fionn, predated Cashel as the seat for the kings of Munster, and after the step sons of Finghin Mac Aed Duibh took the kingship from their uncle Failbhe Flann Mac Aed Duibh, Failbhe's people

came to settle in Knockgraffon. They became the O'Sullivan clan and lived in prosperity there till the Norman Invasion in the twelfth century, when they were pushed west and south. Today though, after 800 years, the Moat of Knock Graffon is once again owned by a Sullivan.

The great Irish historian Geoffrey Keating was parish priest in Knockgraffon around 1610. I wonder, were there versions of this story to be heard then?

LUSHMORE

It is one of those wonders of life that we are all born different: some taller, some smaller; with blue eyes or brown eyes or green; with curly hair, straight hair, fair, brown or black hair. Some of us are great athletes and can run and jump or hurl, some need aids to move around, wheelchairs or walking sticks; some of us have great eyesight or hearing, others use their fingertips to see, and some can't see or hear at all. We each have some great gift to share with the world, be it singing, dancing, drawing or writing, gentleness, leadership or an ability to nurture, console and comfort. And equally we all have some limitation which challenges us in our lives. Sometimes our limitations can be invisible, a lack of understanding, impatience, low self-esteem; sometimes it can be something more visible.

For one man living in the Glen of Aherlow in County Tipperary his limitation was very visible; from the time of his birth he had had a hump on his back. He walked in a funny manner and leaned over to one side because of it. There were things others could do which he found difficult, and some things he would never be able to do at all. But as great as his limitation was, so too was his gift to the world great, for this man had a very positive, uplifting outlook on life and was rarely out of sorts. While some were shy of him because of the way he looked, he got on well enough in his town. He had a great knowledge of local herbs and remedies and a great skill in weaving and plaiting the local rushes into hats and caps and baskets. His work was of a very high quality, and people would pay more for his hats and baskets than other similar work and so he made his living by selling them around in the local towns and villages. He was known locally as 'Lushmore' because of the sprig of foxglove also known as fairycap, which he wore in his own plaited cap, the Irish name for foxglove is *Lusmór*, Lushmore.

One evening Lushmore was returning from Cahir along the road to Cappagh. He walked slowly because of the hump on his back, he could walk no faster and, tired and weary, and thinking of the long road ahead and how he would be walking all night, he stopped for a rest beneath the old moat of Knockgraffon. It was still and quiet and the moon was rising. After a few minutes Lushmore became aware of music, music the like of which head never heard before, like the sound of a great choir singing all together. Lushmore listened intently and picked out the words of their song:

'*De Luain, De Mairt, De Luain, De mairt, De Luain, De Mairt.*'
day loon, day mart, day loon, day mart, day loon, day mart.
Monday, Tuesday, Monday, Tuesday, Monday, Tuesday.

Then there would be a pause and the song would repeat again. Lushmore looked around, trying to work out where the singing was coming from and he realised it was coming from within the moat itself. It was the fairies singing. He listened to the music again enjoying the melody but after a while he started to get tired of the same melody repeating, then a pause and it repeating again. Listening to the tune he could hear on his ear where the melody should go, so the next round he joined in with the hidden choir, singing:

'*De Luain De Mairt De Luain De Mairt De Luain De Mairt ...*'
And when the choir paused he added '... *agus De Ceadaoin*' (day

kay-deen – Wednesday). When the tune repeated again he sang his addition again.

The fairies were delighted with the addition and whisked Lushmore from his sitting place to within the moat. He found himself surrounded by the little people, they sat him up in pride of place beside the musicians. He was brought food and drink and treated like a king. Lushmore was in awe, the fairy kingdom beneath the moat was more beautiful than he had words for, but he noticed a group of the fairies talking among themselves and he was frightened; the fairies had great powers and he wondered what they were going to do to him. They might be angry with his interfering with their song.

One of the group stepped forward. They thanked Lushmore for his addition to their song and added:

> 'Lushmore Lushmore
> Doubt not nor deplore
> For the hump which you bore
> On your back is no more
> Look down on the floor
> And view it Lushmore.'

With that Lushmore felt a great lightness about him and when he looked down at his feet there he saw his hump, having tumbled down from his shoulders, roll across the floor to the other side of the room. He straightened himself up, and looked all around him, everything he saw and heard seemed more and more beautiful. They sang a few more rounds of the song together and later on Lushmore, feeling exhausted, fell asleep.

When he awoke he found himself outside the moat in the early morning. He got up and continued his journey home. Passing through the villages and towns where he was known, he had a job to convince the people that he really was Lushmore, for this tall straight man looked nothing like the Lushmore people had known with the hump on his back.

Word of course spread about Lushmore's meeting with the fairies and how they had taken the hump from his back. It reached the ears of a woman in County Waterford whose friend had a son who had been born with a hump on his back. She made the long journey in search of Lushmore to find out if the story was true and if so, might it be of any help to her friend and her son. She stopped at the house of a tall, straight man to ask for directions.

'Excuse me sir I'm looking for the home of a Lushmore who had a hump on his back but had it removed by the fairies.'

'Look no further,' said Lushmore, 'For I am he, and the fairies indeed did take the hump from my back.'

'Well,' said she,' There's a friend of mine whose son was born with a hump on his back as well and it'll be the death of him soon. I was wondering if the charm that worked on you might work on him too.'

Lusmmore was a good-natured fellow and if he had something that could help someone else he was only too willing to share it. So he told the woman the whole of his story about the place on Knockgraffon where he sat, the music he heard, the line he added, the whisking into the moat, everything. The woman thanked him and headed back to Waterford.

Mrs Madden (for that was the friend's name) was delighted to hear the story, but her son was not like Lushmore. He was a sulky sort, always complaining about everything and cunning and conniving. People around had learned to keep away from him. Mrs Madden put her son up on a cart and brought him across the country to see the fairies at Knockgraffon that he too might have his hump removed. They arrived at the moat and there she left her son by the side of the road on the edge of the moat, to do as Lushmore had done and earn the reward.

Jack Madden sat on the side of the moat and as all became quiet he began to hear the strains of music coming from the moat.

'De Luan, De Mairt, De Luain De Mairt,
De Luain, De Mairt is De Ceadaoin.'

Jack Madden listened a short while and as soon as he was sure it was the fairies he was hearing he blurted out:

'Deardaoin agus De hAoine'.
Deer-deen aw-gus day hee-nah
Thursday and Friday.

If one extra day had worked for Lushmore then surely two extra days might get Jack Madden an extra prize – well such was Jack Madden's reasoning anyway. But Jack had made no effort to appreciate the music of the fairies, he hadn't listened for a suitable place to insert his extra words, nor tried to harmonise with the melody already there. The fairies were not happy he had spoiled their tune. They whipped him up and brought him within the moat, but Jack Madden was not given pride of place. He was not served with food and drink and he did not receive a warm smiling welcome. To the contrary, Jack Madden saw about him hundreds of scowling faces, and one of the group came forward and said:

'Jack Madden, Jack Madden
Your words came so bad in
The tune we feel glad in
This castle you're had in
That you're life we may sadden
Here's two humps for Jack Madden.'

With that, twenty of the strongest fairies brought Lushmore's hump and placed it down on Jack Madden's back, and left him outside the moat again to await his mother. When the mother and her friend arrived the following morning to collect Jack, they found him in an awful state with the two humps on his back, firmly fixed and no chance to remove the new one. The two women lifted Jack back onto the cart and got away as fast as they could afraid that if they didn't they might just find a hump deposited on their own backs.

There is now a camping site near where the moat is. Maybe if you were to camp nearby you might hear the strains of beautiful singing of the fairies coming from the moat. Be warned though: listen you can, but it might be wiser not to join in their song.

Sources
Fairy Legends and Traditions from the South of Ireland by Thomas Crofton Croker (1825); local websites

16

BILL MORONEY'S DREAM

Nearly 500 years ago, Bill Moroney lived in a place called Bothairín Buí not far from Tipperary town. He had a nice little mud-wall cabin thatched with straw and often rushes.

The neighbours would call in visiting or *ag cuairdíoch* nightly and it's many a hair-raising story was told at Bill's hospitable hearth: people that were seen after death, fairies, houses built on the paths frequented by the 'good people', pishoges and superstitions. But the thing that annoyed Bill was to hear people telling of dreams they had. You see, Bill had never had a dream and he always said he would give the world to dream. He was advised to go to the Galtees, where there lived an old wise woman; she, surely, would be able to help him and tell him what way to lay in the bed so that surely he would have some sort of a dream before morning.

One morning, bright and early, Bill set off to walk to the Galtees. There were no trains or planes nor cars in those days and only the gentry had fine horses to ride about on. Bill, like most of the men of his time, had to walk to wherever he had to go and like most of them too he was a fine walker. At that time Bill worked with Sir Charles Doherty, one of the landed gentry and a great friend of Catholics. When Sir Charles had letters to send to England or other foreign countries, it was Bill's job to take them to the quays and put them aboard the ship sailing to those places.

After some time, and an up hill-climb, Bill came to the butt of the Galtee Mountains and there he found the old woman he was searching for. He told her his story of never having a dream and asked what to do about it. She sent him home with an answer, but the answer was a puzzle to Bill and it took him a number of days to figure it out. She told him he should find a place where no one had ever slept before and that he should put his bed there. Bill thought and thought of where he could put his bed, but it seemed to him that every place he thought of someone had slept in at some time or other. One night though it came to him, the neighbours had come *ag cuairdíocht* – visiting, and when the stories and songs were over and all had gone home and the fire was dying in the grate, Bill thought of a place where no one could have slept before.

'I have it!' he cried and he slapped the palm of his hand so hard against his thigh that he sent the poor cat scampering through the door. Bill raked out the fire in the big open hearth and there he put his bed for the night, surely this was somewhere no one had ever slept before. Bill climbed in to the bed and it was not long until he was snoring. He did dream that night and this is what he dreamt:

Sir Charles sent him to carry the mail to Waterford. Bill stopped at the hill of Kilfeacle to have a smoke and a rest and out popped a fox and whipped Bill's bag of letters into the hole. Poor Bill was troubled now. He tramped to Mount Buis and brought two fox terriers back to Killfeacle to rescue the bag of letters from the fox. He succeeded and travelled on again, but the delay was too great, and as Bill was nearing the quays in Waterford he heard the hoot of the ship signalling that she was ready to go, the gang plank was up and poor Bill was left staring after her with his bag on his back.

He noticed a darkening in the sky and looked up, there he saw a great eagle soaring in the sky.

'What's up Bill?' asked the eagle, Bill told his tale of being delayed and missing the boat and he trusted by Sir Charles to get his letters on the boat to England.

'Here,' said the eagle, 'Take my leg and I'll bring you right over the ship and you can drop your bag onto it.'

Bill did as he was told but every time that Bill was about to drop the bag the ship would be gone from under him. Still he held on to the leg of the eagle. Finally the eagle got tired and cross. He ordered Bill to let go of his leg as he could not keep him up any longer.

'If I do, I'll be drowned,' said Bill and he still held on and wouldn't let go. In an effort to shake Bill off the eagle flew up high through the clouds with Bill still hanging on. Looking into a space between the clouds Bill saw three men threshing with flails. 'For the love of God help me!' pleaded Bill. One man put down the end of his flail which Bill caught hold of and held on to for all he was worth. But the thresher was making poor progress of pulling Bill to safety. Finally he got tired of holding him up and he called to Bill to let go.

Bill refused, 'I'll see that you will,' said the thresher and he took out his knife to cut the gad of the flail. Bill saw how perilous a position he was in and with the fright he woke up to find himself clinging on the big old sooty chain which usually hung from chimneys to hang the pots on. He got up from his sooty bed and said a prayer, a prayer that he would never dream again.

Sources
Bealoideas, Iml 4 Uimhir 3 (1934), pp.284–285, collected by Martin Burke from Sean Power

17

WILL HANDRAHAN THE FAIRYMAN

Will Handrahan was born around 1710 in Kilcash. He was the youngest of three children and quite sickly but he was clever. When his older brothers would be discussing their school work or reciting pieces for their father Will would be listening and taking it all in. The neighbours had nicknamed him *Will na Sidh* – Will of the Fairies and his mother used to keep a close eye on him, afraid he might be taken away.

When his mother wasn't watching, Will used to slip out of the house and go walking around Kilcash, he loved being out among the flowers and animals. One time, when he was about seven, he was near the quarry in Dal Cap when he heard music coming from Sleivenamon. He listened and following the music came a wondrous sight. There in the quarry were hundreds of 'little people' and they had tables set with food, there were musicians playing and people dancing. Will was delighted. He slipped into the feast unnoticed and sat there enjoying the sights and sounds.

Suddenly footsteps could be heard and the little people stopped and then quickly all moved through a crevice in the rocks. Will went with them, into a cavern in the mountain. The cavern was huge, and more splendid than Will could ever have imagined. Will was there sometime before the fairies noticed him among their number.

They met together and took council before asking Will what he wanted to do.

Will knew what he wanted, he wanted to remain in the mountain with the fairies, and it was agreed he could stay seven years. Will was delighted. He stayed with the little people, learning from them – he learned all there was to know about herbs and plants, he listened to their music and learned their dances. Soon the seven years had passed and Will was brought before the Fairy Council again to be released. But he didn't want to be released, he asked to stay on another seven years. This was agreed.

Sometimes Will would accompany the fairies when they went above ground on one of their hunts. It was during one of these jaunts that Will first saw Norah Cavanagh and she caught his heart; if ever there was a reason for Will to leave the fairy realm and re-join those on the surface Norah Cavanagh was it. And Will was becoming anxious to leave the fairy realm. It was becoming clear to him that the fairy king's daughter Papenella was falling in love with him, and he could not return that love.

One time when Papenella had turned herself into a butterfly to fly among the flowers on the surface a young boy threw a stone at her and injured her. The young boy was hit with a force field which threw him to the ground and I'm sure he never knew what hit him. Papenella was whisked away and Will was sent for to look after her and make whatever remedy was needed. Papenella played up on the feeling poorly part just to keep Will near her. Papenella's father, the king of the fairies, could see that his daughter was falling in love with Will, and decided he would be quite happy to have Will for a son-in-law. Will realised that it was time to move.

Late one night he arrived at his parents door. His mother sat by the fire, crying and lamenting the loss of her son, as she often did. Her husband had often tried to get her to let it go and forget about it, Will was gone and that was it; there was nothing more they could do about it. They had searched everywhere there was to search all those years ago and maybe he was in a better place. But the poor woman wouldn't let it go. 'My son, oh my son!' she cried, 'I had hopes and dreams for him and they'll never be realised.' Her husband had given up on her, and by now had learned to leave her to have her cry for a few moments and that she would then be all right again. By this time all the other children had grown up and moved away and there was just the two of them in the house.

On this particular night when they were alone they heard a knock at the door. When they answered it there was a young man, dressed in strange clothes but with something familiar about his appearance. Mr Handerhan thought that maybe it was a cousin from across the hills come to visit. They invited the stranger in as that was the way in those times, and sat him by the fire. Then Will told them who he was, and that he had come home. Will's mother was overjoyed. His father was a little doubtful but Will spoke about his brothers, and recalled some events from their younger days and he became convinced.

'I always knew the fairies had an eye on you,' his mother said.

The neighbours all called around and for the next week or two you'd hardly get standing room in the little house for the amount of people gathered there, eager to hear Will's story. But Will was very slow about revealing anything much about his life in the fairy realm. He had been treated well and had enjoyed his time there and he wasn't about to betray the fairies. Norah Cavanagh was among the neighbours who called, and Will was not slow about getting to know her. Soon there was news that the two of them were to be married.

Papenella was not happy about this but there was nothing she could do about it. Will and Norah were married and they were very happy, for a while, then Norah took sick. Will tried every remedy he had learned with the fairies to try and cure her but none worked.

One night, when Norah was not too good, a young beggar woman and her baby called. Will brought them in to sit by the fire and gave them something to eat. The beggar woman stared and stared at Norah in the bed. She told Will that her baby was very sick and they were living in a place and situation that it was clear that they would both die if she didn't find help, she said that she had a dream, in that dream a woman told her to take a journey.

'Sure that's the woman there that appeared in the dream,' she said, pointing at Norah.

Will realised that the woman was meant to come to them, he told her to stay with them until he had found a cure for the baby and he went walking in the fields and hills to collect herbs and plants. The baby was cured after a time and the young woman went her way. Things weren't so good for Norah though and she eventually died. Will was heartbroken. He continued living on in their little house alone and people would come to him for cures and remedies, and his fame spread as a maker of medicines.

It wasn't just in the making of medicines that Will gained fame, he became known for intervening in fairy matters as well. There was a man named Paddy Gallagher who had a fine horse, this horse was his pride and joy and everywhere he went the horse went too. Paddy kept it brushed and washed and looking fine. One day he was returning from the fair at Cahir, having sold his pigs and feeling pleased with himself. On the road he met two men, they asked him would he sell the horse.

'Oh no!' said Paddy, 'No, he's not for sale.'

'You'll swap him then,' said the two men

Again Paddy refused.

'You'll be sorry,' said the two and they moved on.

Paddy continued his journey home and reaching home called to his wife to get the hay for the horse. The wife came back with the hay, but gave a shout when she saw the horse.

'What happened to the horse?' she cried.

Paddy turned to look at the horse and he too gave a little cry, there in the place of his fine strong horse was an old weak nag, worn and tired and just skin and bone to look at.

Paddy turned back to his wife and she gave another start, 'Who are you?' she cried.

'I'm your husband Paddy, what are you on about woman?' replied Paddy.

'Oh no you're not,' said the wife, 'You look nothing like my Paddy.'

Paddy went into the house and saw that he looked nothing like himself: his hair was white and he was old looking. His wife gave him something to eat and something to drink but she wouldn't let him anywhere near the bedroom and Paddy found himself sleeping in the barn that night.

The next day he took a walk through the town and saw some of the men he knew. He called out a greeting to them but they all acted as if he was a stranger. Some asked who he was that he knew their names but they didn't know his. Paddy was feeling awful, he didn't know what he should do. Then he met Will Handerhan.

'Good morning Paddy,' said Will.

'What?' said Will, 'Do you know me?'

'Of course I do,' said Will.

'How is it you can see me as myself and no one else can?'

Will brought Paddy to his house and asked to hear the whole story. Paddy told Will all that had happened to him. Will got up and mixed some herbs and things together. He gave the potion to Paddy and he drank it. Then Will got a piece of paper and scribbled something on it.

'Make sure you go to the fair at Callan,' said Will, 'And that you take the horse with you. When the two men come up to you and ask to buy the horse say no, but that you'll swap him. When they ask what you'll give alongside the horse clap this piece of paper in the hands of the one who asks.' He gave Paddy the piece of paper.

Paddy returned home that afternoon, not knowing what his wife was going to do, but she ran to greet him.

'Oh Paddy, Paddy!' she said, 'Where have you been, there's been a strange man here claiming to be you.' Paddy told her the story.

The following week Paddy went to the fair at Callan taking the old worn, skin and bone of a nag with him. Sure enough, the two men were there, and they approached Paddy.

'Will you sell the horse?' they asked.

'No,' answered Paddy, 'But I'll swap him.'

'What will you give alongside him?' asked one of the two.

Paddy had the piece of paper ready in his hand. He clapped it into the palm of the one who had asked. Immediately his horse changed back into itself, and Paddy never had a problem from the fairies again.

Will often thought about writing down all he had experienced with the fairies, especially all the cures, but anytime he went to write it down his pen would run dry or the ink would spill. Only for the memories of the neighbours he might be forgotten altogether.

Sources

Will Handerhan the Irish Fairyman and Legends of Carrick by John O'Neil (1854)

18

THE FIRST EVER BROGUE MAKER

Did you ever wonder who first had the idea to make *brogues* (shoes)? Or when the first shoes were made? And did you know that the first shoemaker was from Carrick-on-Suir?

There was a time when people had no shoes. Now this was long ago: long before Cromwell came, taking the roof from the old abbey to mend the bridge into Carrick; long before the Danes came plundering and robbing. It was a normal thing then to have no shoes; sure no one had shoes so no one knew any better. People got on with what they had to do but maybe they avoided the rocky roads and pebble shores a little.

There was a young man living near Carrick at that time of the name of Sean O'Dwyer. He was at a house dance one night when he saw Eileen Phelan, and she captured his heart. He asked Eileen out to dance and the two of them were dancing away mightily.

Now there was another fella at that dance. *Capeen Derg* he was known by – red cap, he was one of the fairy people and he had had an eye on Eileen himself. He was mad with jealousy watching Sean and Eileen fly around the room, but he could do nothing about it. He had been planning to tell Eileen that night that he loved her, but up to that time he had never spoken to her and there was no promise between the two of them. Sean had done nothing wrong in dancing with her and *Capeen Derg* had no right of complaint.

Out of sheer spite, *Capeen Derg* got a thorn and, unseen by the room, placed it on the floor where Eileen was dancing on a spot where she would step on it.

Down came Eileen's little white bare foot on the thorn, there was a cry of pain and down went Eileen on the floor. Sean helped her over to sit down and others came to remove the thorn. Where could such a thorn have come from? The woman of the house had swept and scrubbed before the dance began. It was clear, though, that Eileen would do no more dancing that night. Sean helped the poor girl home, as she limped along trying to keep her sore little foot off the ground. Sean left her at her father's door and continued his way.

As he walked, he mused over the question of where the thorn came from and how it got on the floor. Eventually he concluded that there had to have been some devilment in the whole event. Just about that time he heard voices. He stopped walking and listened carefully. He followed the sound and there in the ditch he saw three little people – leprechauns, chatting and working away. Sean wasn't too sure what they were working on. They had little pouches of skin pulled over a wooden implement and they were stitching and sewing and chatting way.

One of the little fellows pulled the pouch off of the wooden tool and put it on his foot.

'Now,' he said to his companions,' There's a brogue for you, and if the girl had been wearing one of these tonight, that thorn of the *Capeen Derg*'s could never have pierced her foot.'

Sean burst in among the three and chased them until he caught one. The other two had disappeared.

'Let me go! let me go!' shouted the leprechaun, 'I'll give you a bag of gold if you just let me go.'

'I don't want your gold,' said Sean, 'Show me how you make one of those things so my Eileen won't hurt her feet again.

'A brogue?' asked the leprechaun, relaxing and flattered that a man like Sean would want to learn his craft. 'No problem.'

The rest of that night Sean watched and listened as the leprechaun took him through all the stages of making a shoe. He was a good learner and the leprechaun enjoyed teaching him. Come the morning he had learned the basics and was set to make his first pair of shoes. Sean was delighted and thanked the leprechaun for teaching him, the leprechaun left him with the tools and implements saying, 'Not a bother, and if ever you need help in the craft just give me a call,' and away he disappeared.

Sean headed back to Eileen's house with the pair of shoes. She was surprised and a little confused until he showed her what to do with them. With the shoes on her feet she would walk about almost anywhere and not have to worry about her hurting her little feet. She was delighted and wore them every day and everywhere, including the following Saturday when she walked down the aisle to marry Sean.

All who saw Eileen's shoes admired them. The priest asked Sean if he would make a pair for his niece and other neighbours followed suit. Soon the entire neighbourhood were walking around in shoes and Sean was kept busy as the only shoemaker around.

No long after this Sean was sent for by the king.

'Sean,' said the king, 'I hear you can make shoes.'

'I can,' said Sean.

'I have a group of neighbouring kings visiting tomorrow,' said the king, 'And I want to impress them. Could you make shoes for me and the queen and all our children?'

'I could,' said Sean, 'But that's a lot of shoes. I'd need help.' With that the little Leprechaun appeared beside him.

'I was up on Sleivenamon and I heard you saying you needed help,' said the little man.

'That's great hearing you have,' said Sean and the two set down to work away together making the shoes. By the morning there were shoes for the king, his queen all the children and the lords and ladies. The king was very pleased. He paid Sean well and kept him close at hand to look after his shoe needs. Sean and Eileen looking back on things later, were quite happy that the *Capeen Derg* had put that thorn on the floor or things might have had a very different ending.

Sources
Will Handerhan the Irish Fairyman and Legends of Carrick by John O'Neil (1854)

19

THE FAIRY PIPE

Seamus O'Flynn was out walking near Gleanaphooca one day, when he stopped for a moment by Gloreagotheen, to take in the old story of how the piper had jumped at the phuca and won the tune from him.

He heard a noise from the bushes and turned to see a little man sitting on the rocks above him, highly amused by Seamus' musings and thoughts. The little man showed no fear of Seamus at all, though Seamus was easily twice his size. He sat on the rock cross-legged, smoking his pipe (or *dhudeen* in the Irish). After a time of them eyeing each other up thus, the little man invited Seamus to sit with him and share his pipe.

Now at this time tobacco was hard to come by, and no one had any idea of the harm smoking might do to a person; it was an activity used to pass the time and bring a little comfort, particularly on those long dark, cold winter's evenings. Seamus didn't smoke very often but enjoyed it when he did. He sat up beside the little man and took a puff of his pipe.

'That is good weed,' said Seamus. The little man only smiled. The two sat together a little longer and then Seamus asked, 'Where could I get some of that?'

'There's a party heading out tonight,' said the little man, 'If you care to come along you can be part of the group and gather your own. It'll last you a good many years if you're careful with it.'

'I'll be there,' said Seamus enthusiastically.

'We leave as soon as the first star shows in the sky. Till then you can keep the pipe and the pouch which will never run out for a year, but mind you don't leave the pipe out of your possession.' The little man disappeared and Seamus sat on, smoking the pipe.

Come first starlight that night Seamus was back at Glenaphooca. Suddenly there appeared all around him little men on horses, all ready for their journey, Seamus was jostled up onto a horse and the party headed off. He didn't know how long they had been riding for and he didn't recognise any of the places they passed through when, just as suddenly as they had all set off, they all stopped. They were in the middle of a cultivated fields where a strange leaf Seamus had never seen before was growing.

'Down you get now, Seamus,' said the little man, 'Help us with the harvest and you can take with you what you can carry.' Seamus got down from his horse and helped in cutting and harvesting the sweet-smelling leaf. He worked for a while and remembered no more until he woke in the morning, sitting on the hillside where he had met the little man. Seamus thought at first he had had a dream, and not a bad one for that, but then he noticed the little pipe he had and the pouch of tobacco, and beside him on the hill was a bundle of the tobacco he had harvested. It had been no dream. Seamus got down from the hillside, went to the rock at Glenaphooca and there he hid away his stash. Then he took himself back into the town.

Things went on normally enough for Seamus, but in the evenings he used to take out the little pipe and his pouch of tobacco and have a little smoke. He wasn't stingy with it either and shared with this neighbours who all appreciated the fine quality of the weed he smoked. Many asked him where it had come from but Seamus kept very close on that and wouldn't give a straight answer, and he was always sure to keep the little pipe to himself and not let it out of his sight. No matter how much he used or gave away the pouch never ran out. Towards the end of a year however, Seamus noticed that there wasn't as much in the pouch as before. It was time to make a trip to Glenaphooca and restock.

Out went a Seamus to the glen again. It was quite and lonely there and he could get to the rock without anyone seeing him. He got to the rock but when he did there was no stash – it seemed someone had got there before him and taken all his leaf. Seamus was about to walk away disappointed when he heard a noise behind him and there was the little man again. He didn't look so good though; his clothes were worn and shabby, he looked tired and worn. Seamus was surprised to see his little friend look so unwell.

'What happened to you?' asked Seamus.

'Ah,' said the little man, 'I used to be the chief of these parts, but the others were none too happy that I had given you that pipe and magic pouch of tobacco nor that I had let you come pick the weed with us. I lost my position and now I'm doomed in service to the pipe and he who has it. So whatever you want I must do for you.'

Seamus felt sorry for the little fellow, and promised himself there and then that he would treat him well and fairly and not ask too much of him. But first he thought ...

'Can you get my store of tobacco back for me?' The little man disappeared and a short time later returned with the parcel of leaf Seamus had gathered almost a year previously.

'Thank you,' said Seamus and he filled up the little pouch leaving the rest of the tobacco in behind the rock. The little man remained standing there, looking sad and sorry, waiting for his next instructions.

'I'm putting you in charge of this store of leaf,' said Seamus, 'and you can use as much of it as you want for yourself.' The little man cheered up a little then.

'And whenever you call,' he said, 'I'll come.'

Seamus headed on then and things continued on much as they had been. Except that Seamus met a girl, a nice girl who liked him as much as he did her. They would have liked to get married but her father was against it. Seamus wasn't well off enough to look after the girl and until he got himself into a good business or got himself a bit of money her father wasn't going to hear about the two getting married. Seamus thought about all kinds of schemes and ways of getting some money. Then the thought struck him that maybe he could set up a little business selling tobacco. He called on his little friend and asked him what he thought of the idea.

'Sure,' said the little man, 'You could do that. Just make sure your little pouch is never completely empty, and be sure you never leave the little pipe out of your possession.'

Seamus headed to the next town and set up a little tobacco business. He did well, the tobacco was of a good quality, and he was fair in his dealings and with his prices. People came from far and near to buy from him. After six months in business he had impressed his future father-in-law enough for the marriage to be allowed to go ahead. Seamus and his wife lived happily enough in their little tobacco shop with the help of their 'little friend' whenever they needed it.

THE PIPES OF FORTUNE

Darby Milligan was a foundling. He had been found on the side of the road as an infant. The whole village had been involved in his up-bringing, each of them taking a turn to house him, feed him, clothe him and teach him, from the most well off of the community to the poorest, and all considered it a privilege to be able to do anything for the wee fellow, for Darby had that type of a disposition that pleases you to please him.

He had taken a strong liking to music and used to follow Tim the piper around learning bits from him and he seemed to show promise on the pipes. So much so that when Tim died the community got together to get the money to buy Tim's pipes from his widow and start Darby off. Darby was very grateful and he played for anyone who asked him. He played at the fairs and crossroads too, sometimes just to please himself, and people would throw him a few coins. Now Darby had never had money before, but now that he had a few coins he found himself wanting more.

He was playing one day on a stone up on the fields when a little man suddenly appeared to him. He was dressed in a green coat and he had bright red hair. Darby stopped playing.

'Oh play on,' said the little man.

Darby played on.

'You are a good player,' said the little man and he took out a new shiny penny, 'Here's a penny for you and there'll be one for you under that stone every time you play here. But mind now, a penny for a tune and don't you ever take the penny without first playing the tune.' Darby took the penny and the little man disappeared. Darby looked at the penny for a while, then he put it in his pocket and played another tune. When he finished he looked down at the stone, there was another shiny new penny. He put it in his pocket and played another tune. He sat there for the evening playing tunes and pocketing pennies. By the time he went home he was too tired to play for the neighbours.

The following day he spent the whole day on the stone, playing tunes and pocketing pennies. By the end of the day he needed to find somewhere to hide his store of pennies. He did the same the following day and, realising he had been nearly two days playing and not a proper bite to eat, he went to get a meal. No one would touch his pipes where they were so he left them on the stone and went or get something to eat.

When he returned there were the pipes, playing themselves and a couple of pennies peeping out from under the stone. Darby was tempted to pocket them for himself but he remembered that he had to earn every penny he got. He took up his pipes, ignored the other pennies and played a tune himself. When he had finished he picked up the new penny he had earned.

So it went on, day after day, Darby played to no one but the stone and earning his pennies. When it rained he built a shelter over the stone, then walls and eventually a house was built around the stone. He had a great deal of money and could afford fine things (a new shiny penny went a long way in those days). He got married to a girl from the next town and settled in with his wife in his house and, in time, had a couple of children. In the night when everyone was in bed, Darby would sit on the stone and play away for his pennies.

Darby had never been a drinker – there used be a saying, 'as drunk as a piper, as sober as Darby Milligan' – but he kept a bottle in the house to be sociable. It happened that in entertaining his guests and his wife's family he grew to like the stuff and began to drink more and more. Soon it got to a stage that you couldn't tell whether he liked the drink more or his money.

One night he woke from a drunken stupor to see his pipes playing themselves on the stone and a couple of shiny new pennies peeping out. Without thinking he reached out and took the penny. A penny he hadn't played for. Suddenly everything went cold and dark. There was his house, wife, family, everything, gone! Darby was alone with just his pipes on the stone in the middle of the field as it had been the first day he met the little man. He cursed himself, his stupidity and he cursed the drink. But what good could that do him now? Darby felt too ashamed to go to anyone who knew him the way things were so he just walked on, away from the stone.

He travelled on till he could go no more. He was cold and hungry but loath to play the pipes as he blamed them for his bad luck. Still he realised he had the means to make a decent living in the playing of the pipes and that alone was something to be grateful for. He shed a few tears remembering his wife and children and then took up the pipes and began to play a sad mournful tune. As he did he felt a weight lift off of him. Out of the corner of his eye he noticed a movement and looking down saw hundreds of little eyes peeking up at him. He smiled, the first smile in what

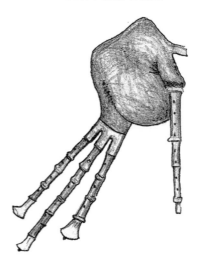

seemed like ages, and played a merrier tune, the little people danced. Darby looked and there beside him was the little man with the red hair who had given him that first penny. He was smiling.

'Well Darby,' he said, 'You're not a bad sort, and when you're sober you're an industrious fellow, but the drink did you no favour nor your miserly ways. You should have shared more and kept less. I'll tell you what though, we'll give you a second chance. Take yourself home now and leave off the hoarding and drink.'

Darby was very grateful. He hurried home and as happy as he was to see the house where it had been, he was happier again to find who was inside it. Mind you, his wife and children couldn't understand why they were getting all the hugs and kisses. Darby was a more generous man after that, and he often had the neighbours around for a few tunes, just a few tunes though and the whiskey stayed corked in the bottle.

Sources
Will Handerhan the Irish Fairyman and Legends of Carrick by John O'Neil (1854)

20

THE YOUNG PIPER

There are many stories about the 'changling', a child left by the fairies in place of a couple's own child which the fairies have taken. The 'changling' is usually a sickly, cantankerous sort and usually in the story the family find a way to outwit the fairies and have their own child returned.

On the borders of County Tipperary there lived a good and decent couple named Mick Flannigan and Judy Muldoon. They had four sons in whom they were proud. Three of them were fine, healthy chaps. But the fourth chap, the third eldest, was the most miserable, cantankerous, ill-tempered of fellows as ever had lived. His hair was shaggy and matted, his skin was greenish-grey, and though he ate more than his three brothers put together, he never had the strength to stand alone nor walk and so kept to his bed.

Judy had a bed made for him close to the fire, that way the young chap would be comfortable. Neighbours when they called or came visiting often saw him there and he always yelped and yowled, screeched and screamed and disrupted them one way or another. Over time they grew concerned that all was not right with the boy and that in fact he might be one of the 'changlings', left in the place of a child stolen away by the fairies or 'good people'.

Now if this were the case, there were a couple of remedies which people had come to hear about and which they were only too happy to advise the parents of. The first was to put the child on a shovel. 'Oh no,' said Judy, 'I can't do that. Put my child on a shovel to throw him on the rubbish heap as if he were no more than a dead cat or poisoned rat. I can't do that.' For as troublesome and ill-tempered as the boy might be, he was still her son and Judy had a mother's heart of fondness for him.

'Well then, you can get a tongs and heat it till it's read hot in the fire, then catch the brat by the nose with it and he'll soon tell you who he really is and where he is from.' But no, Judy wouldn't hear of that either. Various remedies and solutions were bandied back and forth, but none which Judy would entertain until someone suggested she send for the priest, a particularly holy priest who lived in the locality, and ask him to come look at the boy. Judy could find no fault in that suggestion and promised that she would do so. But one thing and then another prevented her calling for the priest and the long and short of it was that the priest never came and things continued on as they had been.

One day, Tim Carroll, the blind piper, called. He sat by the fire, chatting with Judy and after a while took out his pipes to play. As soon as the pipes began, the young fellow who had been lying in his bed by the fire, sat up and began twisting and turning to the music, grinning and kicking his legs. At last nothing would do but he wanted a go of the pipes too. Judy asked the blind piper if he would let her son have a go of the pipes. Tim, who was kind to children, was only too happy to pass the pipes across to the young chap and Judy took them to help fit her son up, but he seemed to know the run of them and was soon comfortably set up. Then he began to play, and he played those pipes as if he had been playing for years. His poor mother was astounded. Tim, blind though he was, could not see the young chap but he could hear the music and he was enjoying it. When he learned that the musician was only five years old and had never seen a set of pipes before he turned to the mother, 'Why mam,' he said, 'What a great joy to you. The young lad is clearly a natural, and if you like I can take him for you and teach him all I know. He has the makings of a great piper and with a little more work, there will not be the equal of him in the whole country.'

I don't think I need to tell you how happy Judy was to hear all that, after her neighbour's worries, to know her son was a natural genius at the music and could have the makings of a decent living as a piper and not have to beg on the streets greatly lifted her heart. As soon as her husband came home she told him all that had happened that afternoon and relayed to him what Tim Carroll the piper had said. Mick too was heartened by the news, for he had worried about his son and what sort of a future he might have. Without hesitation he brought the pig to the fair the next day, and, having sold it, set off for Clonmel to order a set of pipes just the right size for the little lad.

A fortnight later the pipes arrived; as soon as the little chap in his cradle saw them he squealed and wriggled with delight, he bumped himself up and lifted his legs and reached for the pipes till, to quiet him, they gave them to him. He got himself set up as if he had been playing all his life and then he played, to the admiration of all who heard him. Word of his playing spread through the neighbourhood and many neighbours called to hear the young lad play. There was not a piper for six counties around who could be found to better him, and his playing of all the locally known tunes – 'Rakes of Cashel', 'An Madarín Rua', 'The Piper's Maggot' – or any of the Irish jigs brought people from far and near. Indeed when he played 'The Fox Hunt' you could swear you could hear the hounds barking and terriers yelping and all the noises of the hunt in his playing so that you fancied yourself there, in the thick of it all. Best of all, the young lad was not stingy with his playing at all and was only too ready to take up the pipes and play if any of the youngsters around came looking for a dance.

But, he had an air of his own he used to play, which none around had ever heard before, and when he played this everything seemed to dance, the pots and pans and bowls on the dresser; even the stools beneath the people sitting seemed to move in time and those hearing

the tune found they had no choice but to get up and join the dance.
Young and old, boy and girl, and they complained that they were
thrown out in their dances, that they got muddled between steps and
people would end up jostling each other on the floor and the young
lad there grinning and chucking and enjoying the bedlam of it all.

The older he grew, the worse he got. Just a year later his mother
came home one day to find him playing and the cat sitting on top
of the dog and the two flying around the floor to the music. Another
time his mother came in from milking the cow carrying a pail of milk.
The young chap began to play his tune and she dropped the pail
clapped her hands to her side and began to dance a jig. In short there
was no end to the pranks he played and the mischief the got up to.

Mick worked for the local farmer Mr O'Riordan, and things
were not going well on Mr O'Riordan's farm. The horse was lame,
the cows were getting vicious kicking over the pails and one end of
the barn had collapsed. He lost a good calf to 'black leg' and some
sheep to 'red water'. Mr O'Riordan took it into his head that that
unlucky child of Mick Flanigan's must be the cause of his misfortunes. He call Mick aside one day and told him of his misfortunes
and his belief that Mick's child was the cause of it all. 'I'd like it if
you'd look for work elsewhere,' he said, 'You're a good hard worker
and you should have your choice of employers.'

'Well, I'm sorry for your misfortunes, Mr O'Riordan,' answered
Mick, 'And more sorry still that you think that you should think
me or any of mine the cause of them. I'll look for another position
as soon as I can.'

The following Sunday Mick let it be known at mass that he was
looking for another position. A farmer who lived a couple of miles
off offered him a position straight away. He was in need of a plough-
man and only too happy to take on a man like Mick. He offered
Mick a house with a garden and work all year around, Mick accepted
the offer and arrangements were made that the following Thursday
the farmer would sent a horse and cart to collect Mick, the family
and their furniture and they all would move to the new house.

That Thursday the horse and cart arrived and Mick and Judy loaded up their furniture and bits and pieces onto the cart. The bed with the young chap and his pipes was strapped up on the top with Judy sitting beside it so as to make sure it wouldn't fall off on the journey. Then, with the cow walking behind and the other children trotting along the side, picking berries for the hedgerows, they set off.

Now the road they were travelling crossed over a river, which you'd nearly forget was there because it was so deep between the two banks under the little stone bridge. That day though it was quite full because of the rain which had fallen in the week previously. The young lad was lying quiet in the cradle until they got closer to the bridge. Up near the bridge you could hear the water though you couldn't see it and the young fellow became quite distressed. He saw that the horse and cart was headed towards the bridge and across the river, he kicked up and screamed and cried out, 'Whist a *leanabh*!'

'Quiet child,' soothed the mother, but the child just cried the more.

'Bad luck to you, you auld rip! What a trick you played to bring me here.' The child grabbed the pipes, gave Mick and Judy a wicked grin and jumped from the cart, down into the water of the river.

The family sprang to the other side of the bridge and looked over, and there they saw him, coming out from under the arch of the bridge, sitting cross-legged on the crest of a little wave, playing away on his pipes as merrily as if nothing had happened. The river was moving rapidly and he was being whirled at a great rate, but he played as fast as the water ran or faster maybe. Down the bank the children and parents ran, following the child but he went faster than they could go and by the time they rounded the bend he was gone from their sight and they never saw him again. The general belief around was that he had returned to his own people – the 'good' folk, to play music for them and maybe that's where he is still today.

Sources
Fairy Legends and Traditions from the South of Ireland by Thomas Crofton Croker (1825)

21

THE BURNING OF BRIGID CLEARY

Are you a witch? Or are you a fairy? Or are you the wife of Michael Cleary?

The previous stories might seem amusing and something from long ago. But belief in the fairies and 'otherworld' was very strong with many people and remnants of that belief are still around today. There are stories told of the tragedies and accidents which befall those who don't respect the fairy folk and the places where they gather and live, and there are many raths still standing because the owners of the land on which stand refuse to demolish them to build roads or improve land. The belief around the 'changling' is that the fairies sometimes took a person to live in their world, replacing them in this world with a withered replica. The 'changling' would eventually die, leaving the true child to live unlooked for with the fairies; that is unless the true child could be freed. Most of the stories are about infants, some of children. Only a few are about adults.

In the stories there are differing ways in which the fairies can be out-witted. There are stories of children who narrowly escaped being taken by the fairies because some element of our world – a thorn or bit of dirt – failed to be removed so keeping them linked. There are stories of babies, cantankerous and strange, who, when threatened with the fire, red-hot pots, or being left on the rubbish heap, would then rush away in a manner unnatural for their age or being and by the next morning be replaced with the true child in the crib. There are stories of people returning years later and in some cases long after all those they knew had died and gone. The fairy 'changling' was usually of poor health, cantankerous and strange and showed an aversion to religion, holy water, and fire. There were concoctions of herbs which were believed to keep them at bay and other lores which might be more localised to particular areas.

In most of the stories, once confronted the fairy 'changling' fled by whatever means and the true person was returned. The child was never actually burned or scalded – just the threat of that was enough to send the 'changling' on its way. This following story is a true story of events which happened in 1895 and is quite horrific. Had the woman proven to be a fairy 'changling' and been replaced by the true Brigid Cleary, we might think of it as a story much the same as the previous stories. But there was no 'true' Brigid Cleary to be returned. The tragedy is that the people concerned continued in their belief, and a practice which they felt would 'free' her, until the woman they had known as wife, daughter, cousin, friend and neighbour lay charred, burned and dead on the hearth before them.

Brigid Boland was seventeen when she married Michael Cleary in 1887. They lived in her home place of Ballyvadlea, not far from Fethard. Brigid had been an independent woman prior to her marriage, working as a dressmaker and millner in Clonmel, and that didn't change after her marriage. She continued making the odd dress and hat from home on her sewing machine and selling the eggs from her flock of chickens, adding to the income her husband earned as a cooper.

After the death of her mother, Brigid and Michael took on the care of Brigid's elderly father Patrick. Patrick had worked as a labourer in his youth and so was entitled to one of the purpose-built labourer's cottages; Brigid and Michael moved in with him. The cottage was right on the edge of a local rath, or fairy mound.

In 1895, the Clearys had been married seven years and had not been blessed with any children. In March of that year, after a particularly cold spell Brigid took ill. She stayed a day in bed and both her father and husband walked the miles to the local town to get a doctor. The doctor came two days later, on 13 March. He said there was no immediate danger and left some medicine for Brigid to take. But her husband was convinced that the Brigid in his home was not his Brigid but a changling left by the fairies. He believed his true Brigid had been taken by the fairies on one of her walks past the rath and no doctor's medicine could restore her to herself. When Fr Ryan came to call, Michael told him that he and the neighbours knew better ways of curing Brigid than the medicine.

Now if you've paid attention to some of the previous stories – especially 'The Young Piper' – you will be aware of what some of these 'alternative' remedies might be. A lot of those remedies were threats, and it was 'usual' that the 'fairy changling' would leave before they were administered and the true being be restored.

They tried herbs that had been sourced across the mountain from Denis Ganey, who was known as a man who had cures for the fairies. These herbs were to be mixed with 'new milk' – milk from a cow who had only just calved. The concoction prepared, the doors of the house were closed while the mixture was administered to Brigid. Waiting neighbours who came to call told of hearing those within calling out 'Away she go. Away she go.' Before the door was thrown open to allow the fairy to leave. This was tried a few times, each time accompanied with a call to dispel the fairy and call back Brigid.

'Away with you!' they cried 'Come back Brigid Boland, in the name of God come home.

Another time they threw urine on her, again to try dispel the fairy from her.

Later they took Brigid from her bed and over to the fire. They rested her body there, close to the fire on the bars of the grate and said the rosary around her. They questioned her, asking her if she were Brigid Boland, daughter of Patrick and wife to Michael Cleary. She answered each question as a sentence, saying who she was. The group present were anxious that this be completed before midnight and it was. Brigid was then returned to her bed.

The following morning Michael sent for Fr Ryan, the local priest, to come and say mass in the house and so expel any remaining evil spirits or otherworld beings who might remain. The priest came and mass was said around 8 a.m. on the Friday morning. He was completely oblivious as to what had been happening in the house and what the family thought was really wrong with Brigid.

That evening, while some of the neighbours were around, Michael got his wife to take some Holy Water. She got up then and sat by the fire with them, though it was said she seemed very wan and tired. The talk that night was of fairies, pishogues and superstitions. 'Your mother went with the fairies,' said Brigid to Michael, 'That's why you think I'm gone with them too.'

Michael then tried the ordeal of bread, the belief being that the fairies can't eat our bread, so if a person can swallow three dry pieces of bread and jam they must be one of us. Brigid in her frail state struggled to eat the bread, she swallowed two pieces but gagged on the third. 'Swallow it, swallow it or I'll burn you,' shouted Michael. During this time others of the family and friends were keeping vigil near the rath, looking out for the returning true Brigid, but she never came. Michael followed through on his threat, throwing the oil lamp on his wife. One of those present in the room called on him not to burn his wife. 'That's not my wife,' he said, 'Watch and you'll see her coming back.' But the Brigid Michael expected never did come through the door nor did the supposed 'changling' return to its own kind, and Michael was left with his wife's charred dead body on the kitchen floor.

Michael and another of the neighbours took the body and buried it in a shallow grave about a quarter of a mile from the house in some marshy ground. It was found there on the 22 March and an investigation ensued. Michael claimed, when questioned, that the corpse was not his real wife he was still waiting for his wife's return.

The story got international attention with reports from the trial printed in Irish, English and American newspapers. Michael Cleary and nine others were charged with the manslaughter of Brigid. He was sentenced to fifteen years which he served and then emigrated to Canada.

Sources
'The Burning of Bridget Cleary' from *Five Years in Ireland, 1895-1900* by Michael J. McCarthy (1901)

22

HUMOUR, WIT AND LOVE

BACK AGAIN

Captain Wilson of Brawfort was magistrate in Thurles and he
never missed a Saturday in court. Dan Wall as a neighbour and
he knew Captain Wilson had an orchard and that he was never
home on a Saturday. So one Saturday he climbed over the orchard
wall, but who did he see when he reached the top only Captain
Wilson himself.

'Where are you going?' said Captain Wilson.

'Back again,' answered Dan Wall, and he jumped just as quick
back over the wall.

HONEY? HONEY

Mullins had a shop in Cashel town. At one time there was a Scottish
regiment stationed in Cashel and one of the officers wanted a pot
of honey. He sent one of the soldiers to get it. The soldier entered
Mullins shop but couldn't remember the name of what he had been
sent for. When Mullins asked him what he wanted he answered,

'Me sent for a message that me forgot but me know his father well enough, he's a short-legged fellow with a brown mossy jacket with a short belt around his body and a sharp sword out of his arse, and he gangs amongst the flowers crying "boo".'

Confused by the soldier's description, Mullins called to his wife.

'Catherine honey, come here and see if you know what this man wants,' he said.

'Yes,' said the soldier, 'that's the blooming thing, honey!'

He got his honey.

Honest Farmers

A man from Two Mile Borris sent his son to sell a cow at the market in Thurles, and a man from Moycarky sent his son to buy a cow at the market in Thurles. The two sons met on the road to Thurles and said one to the other, 'What brings you here?'

'I'm selling a cow,' said the other to him.

'My father sent me to buy a cow,' said the first, 'If yours has milk she'll do.'

After examining the cow, the two sons struck a bargain and the son selling the cow sold it to the son buying and off went each happy that their day's work had been concluded early in the day and each happy that they had both paid and received a fair price. The two sons returned to their fathers to report on their days proceedings.

The son from Two Mile Borris returned home and showed his father the price he had received for the cow.

'You've robbed that man,' said the father, 'Go back tomorrow and return part of the money.'

Meanwhile the son from Moycarky returned home and showed his father the cow and told how much he had paid for it.

'You've done that farmer,' said the father, 'That cow is worth more, go back tomorrow and pay so much extra.'

The following day the two sons met again, said the first, 'My father said I should return this money to you, you paid too much for the cow.'

Said the second, 'My father sent me to give this money to you, we didn't pay enough for the cow.' Well the two boys took to arguing, neither wishing to return to the father without having handed over the money they had been told to give and neither willing to accept the money offered by the other.

After a while a priest passed the two and stopped to ask what they were arguing about. Hearing the story he turned to each,

'How much have you got?'

'This much.'

'Give it here to me,' then he turned to the second.

'How much have you got?'

'This much,'

'Give it here to me. Now, go home the two of you and don't let ye be found arguing on the road like this again,' and so the two boys went home and that was the end of the matter.

How Ryan Got Polloughs

In winter Polloughs of Inch is a big splash of water and not much of a place to look at. There was a Cromwellian soldier who was given 200 acres of it in payment for his services. When the time came for him to take possession of it he headed out the road to see what he had been given.

On the way he met a man by the name of Ryan on a white horse.

'Where is Polloughs of Inch?' asked the soldier. Ryan pointed out the dreary looking place they were standing in.

'Is it that damn swamp I got?' asked the soldier in disgust.

'That's it now,' said Ryan, 'Make the best hand you can of it.'

'Let me have your old nag and a few shillings to get to Waterford,' said the soldier, 'and you can have the swamp.'

Ryan made the trade, handing over the horse and whatever money he had in return for the deeds of Polloughs. In the winter it may have been covered in water and looked like a swamp but in summer it was good land.

Love in Fethard

I'm sure many people have fallen in love in Fethard, but it's the unlikely stories, the stories of near loss or unrequited love which catch our attention most. This one is from the 1600s and concerns a penniless orphan and a young soldier.

The area around south County Tipperary was very suitable for the keeping of horses and there were four cavalry regiments in the area in the 1600s; one in Fethard and the others in Cahir, Carrick-on-Suir and Clogheen. Robert Jolly was a young soldier stationed with the Calvary regiment in Fethard. He met Eleanor Meagher there, they got to know each other and fell in love, but before he had a chance to marry her he was moved and re-stationed abroad.

There was little hope that Eleanor would ever see her love again. She got work where she could and worked well so that she moved up to better positions, eventually getting a position with a wealthy lady who brought her to London with her as a companion. In London she mixed in wealthy circles, accompanying her mistress to many events and functions. She caught the eye of an elderly wealthy Jew and she married. She was dazzled by the jewels and riches, which she could never have imagined living an orphan life in Fethard. She wasn't married long before her husband died, leaving her a rich widow. Riches however are no replacement for love and Eleanor was very lonely. She would take long walks to try alleviate her loneliness and boredom. One day while walking she passed by barracks and who should be stationed there but Robert Jolly. The two were delighted to be reunited and it wasn't long before they were married. Eleanor and Robert returned to Fethard where they settled near Knockelly Castle. They were both buried in Holy Trinity church where the epitaph on their gravestone stands a testament to their story.

A CHANCE MEETING WITH DEAN SWIFT

Sometimes the story behind how a story was heard or learned can be just as good as the story itself. This story came a long about route to my ears, but for that I enjoyed hearing the story as I am sure you will too. Those involved in the story were from south Tipperary and they told the story to friends and neighbours, as would be expected. Those friends and neighbours passed it on; fathers to sons, until it came to the ears of one Mr Synge who was land agent to the Bagwell's of Marlfield near Clonmel. It happened that one time when Philip Henry Bagenal was visiting the Bagwell's, he heard Mr Synge tell this story. Philip Bagenal then related the story in a letter to his nephew Hope Bagenal, who was serving with the 27th Field Ambulance 9th Division at the front during the First World War. The letter was sent on 24 May 1916 and was received by Hope. He kept it among his possessions and commented on it later. My uncle came across the letter when researching into the Bagenal family of Bagenalstown and so the story came to me, nearly 100 years after the letter was sent. I wonder if in 100 years time they will be resurrecting emails and tweets sent by our generation and finding nuggets of treasure among them like this one.

One time Dean Jonathan Swift, author of *Gulliver's Travels* was travelling through the wilds of Tipperary. There were no cars or trains in those days and he mustn't have been travelling by carriage for a thunderstorm broke and the Dean stopped to take shelter under a large tree there. He was not the only one taking refuge under the tree for a tramp and his female companion were sheltering there too.

The tramp and his common-law wife had been together some years and she had often asked him to marry her and make an honest woman of her. He had put it off and off but now, finding himself in the company of the Dean, sure when would there be a better opportunity? The tramp turned to Dean Swift and asked for his help. The Dean expecting to be asked for alms or charity was surprised when the couple then asked for him to marry them. Hearing their story the Dean agreed and married them there and then. The tramp's wife was delighted as was the tramp and he asked the Dean if he could put in writing what he had done that he might use it as proof of their marriage. The Dean consented and wrote the following lines:

'Beneath an oak in snowy weather
I married this rogue and his whore together.
No power save that which rules the thunder
Can pull this rogue and his whore asunder.'

The tramp held onto that piece of paper and so the story came to be told.

Sources
Back Again: NFC 700, p.32, collected by Seosamh O'Dálaigh from Joe Fannin, age 79, Two-Mile-Borris, 1940
Honey? Honey: NFC 700, p.43–44, collected by Seosamh O'Dálaigh from Joe Fannin, age 79, Two-Mile-Borris, 1940
Honest Farmers: NFC 700, pp.91–93 collected by Seosamh O'Dálaigh from Ned Gorman, age 75, Littleton, 1940
How Ryan Got Polloughs: NFC 700, p.50–51, collected by Seosamh O'Dalaigh from Joe Fannin, age 79, Two-Mile-Borris, 1940
A Chance Meeting with Dean Swift Source: Bagenal Letters

23

PARDON

Once there was a priest called Fr Hogan who was having a new house built for him. The priest had agreed to provide the workmen with a sup of milk each day as they worked. The problem was that this was November, when most of the cows were dry and there wasn't much milk around.

That Sunday the priest put a call out from the altar that if anyone would give him the milk he needed they'd be twice blessed. No one came forward but after mass a new arrival to the town an old farmer by the name of Brien said he'd loan the priest his milking cow and that should do him.

'Thank you very much,' said the priest, 'I'll pay you back double.'

Now there were other neighbours gave what they could. Miss Lahy from Tobaradeora gave him a little pig, which the priest named 'Pardon' and kept to fatten up and the two Miss Coleman's gave him a little bullock calf. That evening Brien brought up the cow and all was well. Or it seemed well, because in the middle of the night the old cow felt uncomfortable and, wanting her usual byre, broke out of the priest's barn and headed home. Farmer Brien was woken up in the middle of the night and had to get up to settle the cow.

Come the morning Fr Hogan sent John, a young lad who worked for him, to see where the cow was. John found the cow at Brien's house and Brien explained what had happened. 'Now,' said Brien,

'I can't be getting up in the middle of the night like this. I'm an old man I'm not able for that.'

John took the cow back and talked it over with the priest. 'We'll tie the bullock and the cow together; that'll stop her wandering,' said the priest. But that night the old cow broke out again, this time bringing the calf with her. Old Brien was woken up again that night but when he saw the calf with the cow he said to himself.

'Well the priest said he'd pay me back double, this must be it. He's finished with the cow and giving me the calf in payment, he'll make a fine meal.' The old man lost no time but slaughtered the calf and skinned it. Later that morning John arrived again, looking for the cow and calf.

'But sure isn't he finished with her,' said Brien, 'Didn't he send the calf as payment.'

'Have you seen the calf?' asked John

'There he is,' said Brien.

'I wouldn't know him,' said John, 'and no skin on him.'

John went back to the priest and told him what had happened. The priest was not pleased and that Sunday he spoke out from the altar telling all the parish to have nothing to do with Brien for disgracing the priest like that.

Brien suffered the isolation for a while then it started to bother him so he came to the priest.

'Father,' he said, 'I've come to ask for pardon.'

'And why should I forgive you after what you've done?' asked the priest.

'Well,' said Brien, 'I've come to ask for pardon, and even Our Lord forgave those who crucified him.' That moved the priest.

'All right,' said Fr Hogan, 'I'll give you pardon, but don't cross me again.' Fr Hogan went on then and Brien made his way to the pig sty and took the pig named 'pardon' away with him.

The following day, John went out to feed Pardon, but the pig wasn't there, he searched everywhere but couldn't find him.

'Father,' he said, 'I can't find Pardon, he's missing.'

'Try that villain Brien,' said Fr Hogan. John went down to Brien's farm, there was Pardon in the front yard.

'I've come for the priest's pig,' said John.

'But I asked him for pardon and he said I could have him', said Brien. There was nothing John could say to that so he went back and told Fr Hogan. The priest was not happy at all and that Sunday spoke off the altar. He condemned Brien and what he had done and told all the parish to have nothing to do with the man at all.

This time Brien suffered. Neighbours passed him by, people weren't talking to him and, to top it all, he was pretty sure his wife was seeing another man. Feeling miserable he decided he'd walk to Ballymore to see his married daughter. He started on the road but halfway there he changed his mind and turned back home. When he got back to the house he heard voices inside.

'The wife had that other fella here,' he said to himself, 'I know, I'll climb up on the roof and see if I can see what's going on down the chimney.' Up he got on the roof and positioned himself beside the chimney to look down. He could hear the voices well enough. Some of the bricks were loose so he took one and threw it down the chimney. It broke a plate on the hearth.

'Bless us,' said his wife jumping, 'Ah 'tis only one of the loose bricks. Pull in here closer to the fire and warm yourself.' Brien heard the two chairs moving and then he could see his wife and the other man clearly. He took a second brick and aimed it at the other man's head. He threw it and it hit the man, killing him dead. The wife didn't know what to do. She took the body and hid it under the bed just before Brien walked into the house.'

'What are you doing here? I thought you'd gone all night,' said she.

'Ah, I changed my mind. Is there any supper?' She got him something to eat and he sat by the fire. The cat was curled up there too. Brien reached out and pinched the cat. The cat leapt and screamed and ran away.

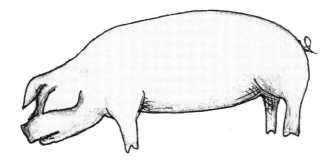

'What did you do that to the cat for?' asked his wife.

'Well, it's because of what the cat's after telling me. He said there's a dead man under the bed.'

'Oh,' said his wife, almost fainting, 'I was going to tell you about that. He just came in to shelter from the cold and a brick fell from the chimney and killed him stone dead.'

'Aye,' said Brien, 'Many would believe you. I'll get the priest now and you can tell him.'

Brien headed back out with the shovel and pick and the body of the man. He stopped at the graveyard at Raygale. Brien dug a grave there and then set the corpse of the man standing in the grave, propped up by the spade so that you would think he was digging it. Then he headed off to the priest's house and knocked on the door.

'Father,' he said, 'Could you come? My wife needs you.'

'Why would I go anywhere for you, you ruffian?' said Fr Hogan.

'If you won't come, I'll go to the bishop and he'll send another priest. In any case it's the wife who is looking for you.'

'All right, all right,' said Fr Hogan 'wait there till I get my horse.'

'Don't bring the horse, something will happen to it and you'll blame me for that too, I'll take you the short-cut through the graveyard.'

'All right,' said the priest. He got his coat and stick and they walked down the lane together. Brien took Fr Hogan through the graveyard and in the half-light they could make out the from in the grave.

'I wonder whose grave he's digging tonight?' asked Brien pointing the figure out to the priest.

'Sir!' shouted Fr Hogan, 'Whose grave are you digging?'

No answer. The priest called again. Still no answer.

'That's terrible,' said Brien as they got closer, 'Imagine not answering a priest, hit him a belt of your stick there father.' The priest hit the man with his stick and the corpse collapsed into the grave. Brien jumped down beside him.

'Father,' he said, 'You're after killing him.'

Poor Fr Hogan didn't know what to do. He tried blessing the man, turning the man, even tried a bit of CPR but to no avail. He was terribly worried.

'Never mind father,' said Brien, I won't tell anybody. It'll be our little secret.' They covered the man over, and from that time on Fr Hogan and Brien seemed to get on better.

Sources
NFC 700, pp.179–187, collected by Seosamh O'Dalaigh from Old Foley, age 93, 1940

24

GHOSTLY GOINGS ON

MAHER'S

There was a house on the Templemore road from Roscrea where a family by the name of Maher once lived. When Mahers were living there they were troubled by strange noises which they only heard at night. Not being able to find any reasonable cause for the disturbances, they were convinced the house was haunted and they decided to sell it. The house was sold and the contents were to be auctioned. Many of the neighbours came to the auction though none of them knew why the Mahers were selling up. There were all kinds of things for sale – house furnishings to bring the women and farm implements to bring the men.

One man came along and bought himself some of the farm implements. He put them into his cart and started the journey home. While he was going along he saw smoke rising from the cart behind him. He stopped the horse and went to the back of the cart. The implements were smouldering but there were no flames to be seen. He tried to put it out but couldn't. He met a woman on the road who had bought a bucket, which was also smouldering. By the time the man got home all that was left of his purchases were ashes.

Maher's auction was the talk of the neighbourhood for a long time.

Treacy's Witch

There was a family by the name of Treacy who lived on the edge of Clonakenny village. Their house was infested by a destructive kind of witch. This witch visited every night but could never be seen; her voice, though, could be heard high in the chimney. People from all parts used to come to the house just to hear her and she would have something to say about each visitor, no matter how far away they had come from. To the Treacy family she was most mischievous, moving things about and such like; there were many times when Mrs Treacy would put a cake of bread in on the griddle to bake only to find it moved into the middle of the floor of the kitchen.

One day the witch changed herself into a hare. A man from the district was out hunting and he rose the hare and he chased it but failed to kill it or catch it. That night he went to visit Treacy's and the voice from the chimney spoke down to him, 'You tried to kill me today but you failed'. Every evening the witch would tell her adventures of the day from the chimney to whoever was listening.

After many years of this a local priest, Fr Vaughan, managed to banish her from the house. The night before she left she said to the family that she would 'Have to go in the morning'. She was never heard in the house again.

Ghost Bride of Sheehil

There was a girl who was getting ready to be married. She had lots of messages to do and the day before the wedding she was in Roscrea, collecting bits and pieces. By the time she had all her business done it was late and getting dark. She was travelling home on her own in her horse and cart, but that didn't bother her as she knew the road well.

Around Sheehill, about 2 miles from Roscrea, at a lonely spot in the road, the cart overturned and she was trapped under it and killed.

At the time of the accident her mother was in their kitchen by the fire and she saw her daughter pass through the kitchen on to her own room. Believing it was her daughter in the flesh she followed her to see how she had got on that day, but there was no sign of anybody in the girl's room. A search party was sent out to look for the girl. They found the overturned cart and the girl's dead body in it.

For years afterwards there were stories about her ghost being seen at the spot where she was killed.

One time a man was travelling that way in his horse and trap when a girl jumped into the trap. He hit out at the stranger with his whip but the whip hit nothing. He took out his rosary beads and began to pray, telling the girl to get out of the trap, 'In the name of God!' People began to become afraid to pass that section of road in the dark. In the end Fr Halpin, a curate in Roscrea, went to the spot to free the girl and banish her from the place. He was successful and she was never seen again. But before she left, she slapped Fr Halpin on the side of the head. When he woke in the morning the hair on that side of his head was white.

HAUNTED HOUSE

Ballintotty and Lisbunny are two townlands which neighbour each other not far from Nenagh. At one time they each had castles in them, the ruins of which can still be seen today. The O'Kennedy's lived in Lisbunny and had a daughter named Ellen who was famed for her beauty and good nature.

The O'Brian's lived in Balintotty but were notorious, especially Donagh O'Brian of whom it is said he killed women and children. One time it is said, he raided a neighbouring area and put all the men and children to the sword and half buried the women in the ground, leaving them to be torn apart by dogs, all just to let his enemies know he would do such things.

Donagh, however, took a fancy to Ellen O'Kennedy who lived with her family at Lisbunny Castle. He asked Ellen to marry him, but she refused and was supported in this by her brother Brian Óg. Ellen's father, hearing Brian's arguments, did not press Ellen to accept the proposal. But Ellen's father got older and eventually died and shortly after her brother was murdered by an unknown hand.

As she returned from her brother's funeral Ellen and her servants were waylaid by Donagh and his men. He killed all the servants and took Ellen to his castle at Ballintotty, where she was forced to become his wife. Ellen was not happy and she died soon after, some saying she fell from her window, though others believe she was pushed from the battlements by Donagh when she confronted him, blaming him for the murder of her brother.

On the second Tuesday of August every year – the anniversary of the day she died – it is said that her spirit revisits that spot.

Spirit Visitor

One night a spirit came into a house and sat in the corner. When the man of that house came home he saw a shadow in the corner, he walked towards it and the spirit spoke. The man got frightened and went into the other room to bed. No sooner was he in his bed than the spirit came into the room and said, 'Will you come out with me, and I will show you where I live.' The man said no, but the spirit took him by the hand and led him to a field then disappeared.

The man returned to his house and found the spirit in his bed. When the man entered his room the spirit left and stood outside the window. In the morning the man woke to find the fire lit, and breakfast ready. The man expected the spirit would visit again, but it never did. But even though the spirit never came to visit again he was never really able to sleep soundly again. He found he was always dreaming of ghosts and fairies.

MULLOWNEY

Mullowney was a man who had come from Clare to work in Tipperary. He came to Two Mile Borris and got work firstly with a family of the name of Weston. Mrs Weston was expecting a baby and one night she was sick. Mr Weston sent Mulowney out for whiskey and other groceries. On the way back Mulowney was passing through the bog. That bog is long cut away now but it was there then. Passing through a gap in the hedge of the bog he saw a tall dark stranger standing over him. The figure changed suddenly into a dog and began to attack him. Mullowney thought he was a goner, when a little Connemara pony on the bog came to his rescue and chased the dog way. The pony lowered itself onto its knees beside Mullowney to let him get on its back, but Mullowney was too shaken for that. He wrapped his arm around the pony's neck and leaned on it all the way home. The pony continued to keep the dog away until they reached the Weston's house.

Mullowney handed in the groceries through the door and went straight to the barn and slept. The next day he went looking for the pony who had saved him. He found the pony back on the bog with only one eye and a lot smaller than he remembered. From then on he kept an eye on the pony any time he was near. Other people had heard stories from that section of the bog too.

Mullowney left Weston's and went to work for a man named Maher. He worked hard for Maher during the week but when Sunday came and he went out hurling and proved himself on the field. That night, after he had gone to bed, a party came with guns, blackened faces and cloaks so no one would recognise them. Mr Maher answered the door.

'What do ye want?' he asked. 'Not you, but the young lad with you,' they said.

Mullowney could hear them from his room. He got out of bed and hid behind the door with a spade and when the group came in for him, he hit them one by one and knocked them out.

The group gathered again outside and decided to shoot Mullowney. They aimed their gun in through the window and began shooting in a pattern around the room. Mullowney inched along the wall, avoiding the bullets but was running out of space. He took shelter in behind a basket of potatoes. One of the shots grazed his shoulder, he let out a cry and the group thought they had killed him so left. The next day Mullowney left Maher's and went elsewhere for work.

He took up with a man named Jimmy Ceasar who lived out in a lonely place on the bogs. One November's night when he was coming down the little bohereen (little road) to Ceasar's a group of men leapt out of the ditch.

'What do you want?' asked Mullowney.

'We want you,' said they, 'Come with us, and we'll do you a good turn.'

They brought Mullowney up the lane towards Hayes farm. Mullowney knew it was their intention to rob the farm and he refused to go any further. He refused to play a part in any robbery. The group took him there and then and made him kneel down by a cart. They took the shaft of the cart and killed him with it, leaving his body in the ditch.

That night Jimmy Ceasar heard a knocking at his door and went to answer it but there was no one there. Then he heard a voice, a voice he recognised, the voice of Mullowney. The voice said to him, 'I'll go under the roof of a house no more. You'll find my body buried in the ditch on the lane, about 2 feet from the turn in the road to the church. Retrieve it and bury it in consecrated ground.'

Ceasar wasn't sure what to do, and as a Protestant he knew none of his neighbouring landowners would believe him so he decided to do nothing.

Many years later, when Jimmy Ceasar was nearing ninety years of age, he was passing down the lane one day while some men were working and they told him they had come across the body of a man. Ceasar asked them if it was in the ditch, about 2 feet from the turn in the road to the church. They were surprised he could be so precise for that was exactly where they had found the body.

LANTHAM'S WIFE

There was a Protestant man named Lantham who lived in a house in Grangemore near Cashel. His wife had recently died and was buried in Ballysheedy. Poor Lantham was stricken with grief and his friends thought it better that he not return to his home alone, where he would be surrounded by reminders of his wife.

They took him to a friend's house to stay for a while, and a servant was sent to Lantham's house to get some things for him. But when the servant arrived at his house, there was the ghost of the man's dead wife, dressed and sitting by the fire. A minister was sent for but he couldn't shift her. Finally the local priest was sent for and he persuaded her to go.

WHERE BILL KEANE LIT HIS PIPE

There was a contractor and pump sinker in Tipperary by the name of Morrissey. Thomas Power's brother used to work as carpenter for him at times. Thomas remembered as a young lad being sent in the winter with the donkey to collect his brother and bring him home. He would wait in Morrissey's kitchen by the fire till his brother came in from his work.

There were two old men, Dick Cooke and Bill Keane, who used to come visiting to the Morrissey house. They were butter carters in their day and had plenty of stories to tell. One night Thomas was there when the two men related this memory.

'Do you remember the night Dick?' said Bill, 'Of the house in the bog?'

'Begor I do,' said Dick, ''twas very strange.'

Mrs Morrissey pressed Bill to tell the story.

'The funny thing is there was no house at all in the bog,' said Bill, 'and yet there was. I and Dick here were going to Thurles one night with two horse-loads of butter. When we got to the Bog of Ballymore Dick said to me, "We had a right to kindle our pipes back the road. There is no house now for the next five miles."

'"Ah sure we must do without our smoke so," said I. There were no matches in those days. We jogged along for a couple of miles more and in from the road about fifty yards – in, *in*, the bog – I thought I saw a rush light in a window. "Hould on Dick," said I, "There's a house here and we'll light up".

'"There's no house here," said Dick. "I travel this road by night and day and I bet you there's no house for two miles more."

'"Wait there a minute," said I, jumping down off the car, "I'm blind if there isn't".

'I crossed over the ditch and struck for the light in the window. It was a nice little thatched cottage with the door open. I said, "God Bless you all" but got no reply. There was a good fire of turf and a man sitting beside it with his elbows on his knees and his head laid in his two hands. I went to the fire and kindled my pipe then turned to come out again. Then I saw that the house was divided by a sort of curtain partition. The curtain was but half drawn and inside the curtain there was a bed with the corpse of a man laid out. I went to the side of the bed and said a prayer for the dead man and left.

'Dick was outside in the yard – he wouldn't light his pipe there at all, and he couldn't be persuaded that there was a house there all the time, and still he was looking at it. I wanted him to come in but, no, he wouldn't. Then he pulled a furze that was growing nearby and stuck it on the side of the road where the house was.

'"I bet you any money when we're coming back with daylight tomorrow there'll be no house there," said he.

'"Yerra go away out of that," said I, "How could I light my pipe so?"

'We continued our journey, unloaded in Thurles and headed back early the following evening. There was still plenty of daylight when we were passing that spot in the bog. There was the furze standing on the ditch where Dick stuck it. But no house nor any shadow of a house. But I lit my pipe there anyway.'

Sources

Maher's: NFC 549, Scoil an Clochar, Roscrea, Barony of Ikerrin, Tipperary, pp.147–9, collected by Philomena Tobin from James Darby, age 74

Treacy's Witch: NFC 548, Scoil Lios Dubh, Dún Chiarán, Ikerrin, p.70, collected by Francis Meagher from Michael Sutton via her mother

Ghost Bride of Sheehil: NFC 548, Scoil Lios Dubh, Dún Chiarán, Ikerrin, p.132, collected by Sorca ní Meacair from her mother

Haunted House: *Fairy Legends and Traditions from the South of Ireland* by Thomas Crofton Croker (1825)

Spirit Visitor: NFC 547, Clonmore School, Killavinogue, Ikerrins, pp.205–6, 'Spirit Visitor' from John Condon

Mullowney: NFC 700, pp.9–17, collected by Seosamh O'Dáligh from Joe Fannin, age 79, Two-Mile-Borris, 1940

Lantham's Wife: NFC 700, pp.36–7, collected by Seosamh O'Dáligh from Joe Fannin, age 79, Two-Mile-Borris, 1940

Where Bill Keane Lit his Pipe: Bealoideas, Iml 4, Uimhir 3 (1934), collected by Martin Burke from Thomas Power, pp.280–1

25

THE
DULLAHAN

The Dullahan is a character in Irish mythology who has no head. Some stories tell of them carrying their heads beside them as they ride along, or in their hands. This story tells of an encounter between a mortal and a walking Dullahan there is a version of it in Thomas Croftan Croker's collection entitled 'The Good Woman'.

At the foot of the Galtee Mountains lived Larry Dodd. He was a man who while trying his hand at farming had his heart in working with horses. He was known for his gift in breaking horses and training them and this had made him a name and the odd few bob among those who hunted in the area.

One evening Larry was returning from Cashel where he had bought a horse on the promise of paying for it soon. He was sure he had bought a bargain and with a little work on the mare he could sell it again at the fair in Kildorrery for a profit, pay his debtors and pocket the rest for himself and his wife Nora. He rode home that June evening in high spirits, thinking that if horses could be bought so cheaply who would be fool enough to have to walk.

While this thought was passing through his head, he passed a woman walking briskly by the side of the road. She was wearing the large cloak usual of the time and so he couldn't tell if she were young or old, but being in high spirits and remembering the saying 'civility begats civility', he offered her a lift on the horse behind him, as far as he was going that was, on her way. He received no reply.

She continued to walk briskly just ahead of Larry, and Larry, believing her non response had come for bashfulness and shyness, moved ahead of her, stopped the horse and alighted. 'Ma'am,' said he, 'Jump up here behind me and I'll bring you safely through this next lonesome bit of the road.' She didn't answer him but must have understood his gesture for sure enough she jumped up on the back of the horse and, Larry before her, they both headed off along the road. 'I hope you're comfortable there,' said Larry, but he received no answer.

They travelled on in relative silence, it getting very quiet as they came to that 'lonesome' part of the road to which Larry had referred. He could see the majestic head of Galteemore in the distance, and hear the odd bird in the fields. Larry could hear too that the horse had a loose shoe which clicked as he was walking on the road. The trees were old along this bit of road and in one place there were a few trees which grew together around a dark pool of water, a place where cattle would be brought to drink. The horse must have been familiar with the spot because as they approached the water she stopped dead in the road.

Larry dismounted, not sure as to how the horse might behave and, not wanting his new charge to end up in the water, he thought it wiser to lead the horse over to the pool for it to drink. Standing there Larry checked the loose shoe on the horse's foot. 'By the piper's luck that always found what he wanted,' said Larry, 'What have I in my pocket? Only a horseshoe nail. All I need now is a suitable stone and I can fix that show myself, it's not the first time nor will it be the last time I've no doubt that I fix a loose shoe.'

He bent down to do the work and as he did the woman jumped down, almost silently, and off she set, without so much as a 'good bye' or 'thank you'.

'What?' called Larry, 'Don't I get to see your face, nor earn a kiss for my help?' And he chased after her. The woman though didn't take the road. She headed up the path through the fields that led to an old ivy-covered church – Kilnaslattery Church. Larry followed after her, and when she jumped over the churchyard wall he kept following, made more and more determined by her seeming stubbornness.

Over the wall jumped Larry after her, landing in a newly dug grave. He got out of that and moved on through the gravestones and old men's bones, the cloaked woman before him all the time. She came up to the old church itself and began to circle around it, she circled it once, twice, and on the third round Larry thought he'd be clever and catch her as she rounded the church and take his kiss. He grabbed her as she rounded the church, turned her towards him and went to kiss her, but, Glory Be, she had no lips, no face, no head!

The blood in Larry's veins seemed to turn to ice. His head was spinning, he could not believe that he might have held a dullahan in an embrace. He staggered into the church and fell in a dead faint. When he opened his eyes he found himself in the middle of a strange spectacle. Larry would have called out for help but his tongue cleaved to the roof of his mouth and he could not speak. He would have run but his body was rigid and frozen. In the centre of the old ruin there was a wheel of torture, like that to be found in Cork Gaol, on which were a multitude of heads and skulls. Larry could hear a bell clanging, a strange sound to dance by, but there around the wheel were well dressed men and woman, soldiers, sailors, priests and nuns dancing to the music and all without heads.

Larry didn't know where to look, he didn't know what to think. 'I'm done for and lost forever!' he cried out.

'Welcome Larry Dodd' called the heads on the wheel. One of the dancers then went to the wheel and taking (what Larry presumed was) his own head off the wheel, put it under his arm and proceeded to offer Larry a brimming cup. Larry, to show his manners drank it down. 'Capital stuff!' he was about to say, but he got no further than 'Cap ...' when his own head was cut off and went dancing about on his shoulders. Larry could not remember what happened next clearly, for it seems having your head separated from your body is not good for the making of memories, but he said there was some cracking of whips and rolling of carriages.

When he woke up the first thing he did was to put his hand up and check his head was still there, and glad was he to find it was, he shook it gently to make sure it stayed on and then looked around to see where he was. He was lying on his back in the middle of Kilnaslatterey church in broad daylight. Maybe it had all been a dream, but Larry could think of no dream that would bring him to Kilnaslattery church in the middle of the night. He got up and made his way back down through the fields to the pool of water beside the road to get his horse and continue home. The horse was nowhere to be seen.

Larry walked home wondering what he would say to his wife. He had bought the horse on the promise of paying his debtors when he sold it again and now he had no horse to sell. More over, how would he explain ending up in Kilnaslattery Church and the dullahan – and losing he head over a girl.

Sources
Fairy Legends and Traditions from the South of Ireland by Thomas Crofton Croker (1825)

26

CARDS WITH THE DEVIL

There are lots of stories of people playing cards with the devil. In some the priest arrives in time to save them from going to hell, in others they manage to out-wit the devil themselves and in others they are taken away and never seen again.

CARDS WITH THE DEVIL

A man from Dromard was always playing cards and some nights it would be very late when he was coming home. One night when he was coming home he met a man on the road who stopped him and challenged him to a game of cards.

'You have a deck there in your pocket,' said the stranger.

So they played together for some time, playing for this and that and nothing of much consequence. Then the stranger said, 'Why don't we play for each other?'

Not really knowing what he meant the man played on but the stranger won that game and he told the man that he would be along to take him soon. The man became afraid then and he went to the local priest and told him the story.

'That stranger was the devil,' said the priest, 'and he'll be coming to take you to hell.'

The priest gathered all the people and the man in a local barn and when the devil came for the man, the priest drove him out through the wall of the barn and the devil never returned.

Windy Gap

Windy Gap is near Nenagh. There was a fellow one time who was always playing cards. He'd be out till late at night or early in the morning with his card playing. One night he was coming home after playing cards and he was half boozed up from drink (they used to play for a half gallon of porter those days). As he was passing the Windy Gap he noticed a fellow sitting on the ditch there. The stranger had a pack of cards with him and he stopped the man and asked him if he would play. Of course the card player was only too glad to begin another hand and he stopped and played the game.

They got to a stage where the fellow on the ditch said to the card player that if the card player lost the next hand he would have to go with the stranger. But the card player didn't think that he could lose so he played on.

There was a priest coming up the road just at that time on his way to a sick call. His horse, sensing that the stranger on the

ditch was no man but the devil himself, bolted and the priest was thrown from the horse. The card player went to his aid but as the priest was getting up he caught sight of the two crubeen (cloven) feet of the stranger. The priest stood up and ordered him to go.

There was a flash of fire and the stranger disappeared. The card player got home safely that night, but he realised how close his end could have been and he never played cards again.

LATE NIGHT CARD GAME

A man named Jack went card playing to a house to the east of Bourney parish. It was late and dark when he was returning home to his own house. He saw a light coming towards him on the road so stepped into the ditch to avoid it. It was a funeral procession which passed him with six or seven men carrying a coffin. When they neared him they laid the coffin down to tighten the cords tying it and one man called to Jack to come out from the ditch and help them carry the coffin. Jack did, and they headed off across a field towards the graveyard.

One of the group stepped away from the coffin and went to a house to get the tools needed to dig the grave. The rest waited some time and when it looked like he was not returning the second man went for the tools. So it continued till there was but one and Jack left. Jack said he would go for the tools and set off … for home.

On the way home he came to a house and he knocked on the door. It was a cold night, and the woman who opened the door invited Jack in to warm himself. Before he had time to sit down, however, she asked him to bring in a basket of turf. He went out to the turf pile and picked up a sod and put it in the basket, but before he had time to pick up a second sod the first had jumped out of the basket and back onto the pile. Jack tried again and again, after a time the woman came out to him.

'You were never any good,' she said, 'And you never will be.' She filled the basked with turf herself and they went back inside.

She asked him then to put the little potatoes into a pot so she could boil them on the fire. Jack picked up the potatoes and put them in the pot, but, as before, no sooner had he put them in the pot than they jumped back out into the sack. As before the woman came, told him he'd never be any good, and filled the pot with potatoes herself.

When the potatoes were boiled the woman invited him to sit at table with her and eat them. She peeled the potatoes left the skin to one side and ate the potatoes. Jack tried to do the same but no sooner had he peeled the potatoes than they jumped back into their own skins again. The woman got fed up with Jack and she chased him out of the house with a mallet.

As he ran down the road, Jack heard a great noise. He turned around to find the men who had been carrying the coffin now chasing after him, full of anger. They were gaining on him and as fast as he was running it seemed likely that they would catch him. Just then the cock began to crow, announcing the approaching dawn. The men disappeared. Jack made it home as well as he was able, and lived to tell the tale another day.

Tom Butler Bests the Devil

Just outside Carrick-on-Suir is the fine residence which Tom Butler built at the end of the sixteenth century. The Butlers got their name from being the bottlers for the King, an official title *'de bottiler'* and they remained the official 'bottlers' up to the 1800s.

Anyway, there is a story that one of the Tom Butlers of Ormand Castle had made a pact with the devil. The devil gave him all the wealth and fame he could want and in return, at the appointed time, Tom was to go with the devil.

Tom became rich and successful and was enjoying his wealth, but as the appointed date neared he was less and less happy about having to go with the devil. On the day that the devil arrived to collect him Tom pleaded for more time. He got it. The devil would give him a year and a day more and then he would have to leave.

Tom enjoyed his year extra but still he didn't want to have to leave with the devil so he came up with a plan. On the day the devil called to collect Tom, Tom was ready. He had a great meal prepared and the place looking warm and cheerful. He treated the devil as a welcome guest, inviting him to come and sit and dine and drink. The best of wine was flowing and the devil readily accepted. They ate and chatted and laughed and drank. Soon they were both in a merry state and Tom asked for more time.

'No!' said the devil.

'Well then,' said Tom, 'Let's have a race, once around the ash grove. If I win, you leave me here and leave me alone. Whoever wins can take the last with him.' The devil agreed.

Out went the two, took their places and prepared to race. They set off. The moon was bright and shining in their faces. The devil easily won.

'Ha ha,' he cried, turning to Tom, 'I won, now you have to come with me.'

'No,' said Tom, 'The agreement was whoever won would take who came last, and he came last,' said Tom, pointing at his shadow.

The devil was furious. He took Tom's shadow and disappeared. Tom lived on unhindered. But, they say, without his shadow he could gain no entry to heaven, and so Tom can be seen now, wandering the grounds of the house, looking for his shadow.

Sources

Cards with the Devil: NFC 547, Clonmore School, Killavinogue, Ikerrins, p.3, collected by Shiela Leahy from Mrs Delahunty

Windy Gap: NFC 700, pp.219–220, collected by Seosamh O'Dálaigh from Mary Hurley, 1940

Late Night Card Game: NFC 547, Clonmore School, Killavinogue, Ikerrins, pp.203–5 from Ben Reeves, age 68

Tom Butler Bests the Devil: *Will Handerhan the Irish Fairyman and Legends of Carrick*, John O'Neil (1854)

PRONOUNCIATION GUIDE

Adh Ladhrann	Aw Lowran
Aengus Mac Nathfarach	Ain-gus Mack Nah-far-ock
Ag cuairdíoch	Egg-coor-dee-ock
Aithirne	Ah-hir-nah
Aodh Dubh	Ay Duv
Aodh Guaire	Ay Gway-rah
Aonghus	Ain-gus
Bachal Iosa	Bock-ol ee-sah
Banbán	Ban-bawn
Bearnan Cuailan	Bare-an coo-lan
Bec Mac De	Beck Mack Day
Bith	Bih
Boilce ban Breathanach	Bwill-cha ban Brah-knock
Boinn	Boyne
Bothán	Buh-hawn
Brugh na Bóinne	Brew na Boyne
Caer	Care
Cainnach	Cawn-ick
Cessair	Kes-sar
Clais Duirdrenn	Claws Deerdreen
Conall Mac Nenta Con	Konal Mack Nan-tah Con
Corca Duibhne	Kurka Gweena

Crimthann Mór Mac Fidaig	crim-hawn More Mack Fih-dayg
Cúchulainn	Coo-kul-in
Cuiririan	Cur-ih-reen
Dal Cais	Doll Caws
Dhudeen	Doo-deen
Diarmuid Mac Cearrbheoil	Deer-mud Mack Carroll
Dubh Tuinne	Duv Tin-ah
Diarmuid Mac Cerbhoill	Deer-mud Mack Carroll
Duirdriu	Deer-drew
Dullahan	Dull-ahawn
Dun Chairan	Doon key-ron
Eathal Anbhuail	Ee-hal On-vwill
Eochy Mac Luchta	Ucky Mack Look-tah
Eoganacht	Oh-gan-awct
Eoghan Mór	Own More
Failbhe Flann Mac Aed Duibh	Fal-va Flan Mack Ay Duv
Faoi gheasa	Fwee Gas-ah
Feradach	Fair-ah-dock
Feidhlim	Fay-lim
Finghin Mac Aed Duibh	Finian Mack Ay Duv
Fionntan Mac Bochan	Fintan Mack Buck-hawn
Foras Feasa ar Éirinn	Fore-us Fas-ah Air Air-in
Gleann Caoin	Glen Queen
Gruibne	Grub-nah
Gobán Saor	Guh-bawn Saw
Guinnegh	Guin-ee
Imleach Iubhair	Im-lock Oo-vir
Ingen Uí Fidhgheinte	Ing-in Ee Fee-yen-tah
Ladhra	Lah-hra
Lathna	Lah-na
Leanabh	Ian-iv
Loch Béal Dragan	Lock Bale Drag-on

Luach Magh	Loo-ick My
Luighteach	Lee-tyawck
Mahon Mac Cinnéide	Mah-han Mack Kennedy
Meagher	Maher
Mobhi	Mow-vi
Mochoinne	Mow-quinn-ah
Muircheartigh	Muir-hir-tig
Naoise	Nee-sha
Oilell	Oll-ill
Odhran	Oh-rawn
Poitín	Put-een
Rachau	Rack-oo
Scath na Leguane	Skaw nah Lih-goon
Slieve Beatha	Sh-leeve Bah-ha
Sliabh na mBan	Sleeve Nah Mon
Slighe Dala	Shlee Daw-law
Sidh ar Feman	She air Feman
Smirdubh Mac Smal	Smeer-duv Mack Small
Samhain	Sough-in
Sidh Uamhain	She Uvwin
Senchán Torpeist	Sen-kawn Tor-fayst
Táin Bó Cúailnge	Tawn Bow Coo-ling
Tathen O'Carroll	Tah-hin O'Carroll
Tonn Tuinne	Ton Tone-ya
Tountinna	Ton-tin-ah

SOURCES AND COLLECTORS

The stories in this book have come from a number of sources: the National Folklore Archives, local history articles in magazines and periodicals, online websites and tourist information. Below are the sources without which this book could never have been compiled. There are also some of the websites and reading materials which may be of interest if you wish to know more.

AIDEEN McBRIDE 1973–

Aideen was born and reared in County Carlow. She came to college in Dublin in the 1990s, married, and is living there still. She works as a storyteller, enjoying the worlds of times past and countries faraway, possible to reach through stories. The first stories she told were the ones she heard from her father and adds to that repertoire with stories collected from local sources and other storytellers. In 2014 she and her father, Jack Sheehan, published *Carlow Folk Tales*. She has also worked collecting stories from across County Carlow which were presented to the National Folklore Archives in October 2014.

THOMAS CROFTON CROKER 1798–1854

Thomas Crofton Croker was born in Cork and had a great interest in Irish folklore. He and his wife collected many stories and recorded many Irish customs and traditions. His 1825 publication, *Fairy Legends and Traditions from the South of Ireland*, was the first time Irish or English oral folklore was recorded in writing. There were six editions of the book, which the brothers Grimm translated into German. The second edition included illustrations by the Irish artist Daniel Maclise.

JOHN O'NEILL 1777–1854

John was born into a poor family in County Waterford. Aged 9 he was apprenticed to a shoemaker and by 21 he was living in Carrick-on-Suir and married. He wrote poetry, songs and plays. In 1854 his collection of stories from around Carrick-on-Suir was published as *Handerhan the Fairyman and Legends of Carrick*. John was very involved in the Temperance Movement and wrote in praise of Fr Mathew.

NATIONAL FOLKLORE COLLECTION

The Folklore Collection housed in UCD is an invaluable resource, housing the Schools Collection from the 1930s and other collections of stories made between the 1920s and today. Many of the collections are in handwritten copybooks which were a pleasure to read through. The archives in Newman Building in UCD are open to the public 2.30–5.30 Tuesday to Friday. For information check the website www.ucd.ie/irishfolklore.

MARTIN BURKE

Martin Burke visited the home of the Powers in Rathkea near Tipperary town in 1932. Mrs Power, Mary Power, Kitty Power and Thomas Power lived in a little farmhouse there and Séan Power lived a short distance away in the town land of Ballinard. Martin recorded the stories they had to tell and they were published as an article entitled 'Tipperary Tales' in *Bealoideas*, lml. 4, Uimhir 3 (1934), pp. 277–91. Most of the stories were told by Thomas, a carpenter, who heard them from his grandfather who died around 1897, aged 104.

SEOSAMH Ó DÁLAIGH

Seosamh Ó Dálaigh was born in the Gaeltacht area of Corca Duibhne in County Kerry in 1909. He trained as a National School Teacher and taught for a while before beginning in 1936 collecting stories and folklore. He collected in Irish and English. It was Seosamh who collected the stories from Peig Sayers on the Blasket Islands. Around the 1940s he spent considerable time in and around County Tipperary collecting material which is available to view in the National Folklore Collection in UCD. Seosamh died in 1992. It is estimated that he collected over 60,000 manuscripts in his lifetime.

SCHOOLS COLLECTION 1937–1938

The NFC are working towards making the Schools Collection available to view online. Scans of the original manuscripts are being uploaded county by county and can be viewed at www.duchas.ie.

BIBLIOGRAPHY

Books

Alban Butler revised by Paul Byrne, *Butler's Lives of the Saints* (Byrnes and Oats, 1998)

Thomas Crofton Croker, *Fairy Legends and Traditions from South Ireland* (John Murray; London, 1826)

William Dooley, *Champions of the Athletic Arena* (General Publicity Service, 1946)

Paul J. Flynn, *The Book of The Galtees and Golden Vein* (Hodges, Figgs and Co., 1926)

Lady Gregory, Lady Gregory's Complete Mythology (John Murray, 1902 and 1904; reprinted Bounty Books, 2012)

Dáithí Ó hÓgáin *Myth, Legend and Romance* (Prentice Hall Press, 1991)

John O'Neill *Handrahan the Irish Fairyman & Legends of Carrick* (Tweedee, 1854)

Revd John O'Hanlon, *Irish Folklore – Traditions and Superstitions of the Country* (Glasgow, 1870)

Richard Sheehan, *Bagenal Letters* (Carloviana, 2010), pp. 48-51

James White, *My Clonmel Scrapbook*, 3rd edition (James O'Connor Knocknagow Bookshop, 1980)

WEBSITES

www.aherlow.com

www.anim.ie

www.ballingarry.net

www.barnanens.scoilnet.ie

www.bcparish.com

www.burncourt.com

www.cashel.ie

www.cashel-emly.ie

www.catholic.org

www.emly.ie

www.fethard.com

www.holycrossballycahill.com

www.justor.org: Conall Corc and the Corco Luigde by Vernam
Hull in *PMLA*, Vol. 62 no. 4 (Dec 1947), pp.892–899 published by
Modern Language Association; 'Loughmoe Castle and its Legends'
by Revd St John D. Seymore in *The Journal of the Royal Society of
Antiquaries of Ireland*, Fifth Series, Vol. 39, no. 1 (1908), pp.70–74

www.libraryireland.com: The Burning of Bridget Cleary from *Five
Years in Ireland*, 1895-1900 by Michael J. McCarthy, 1901

www.loganim.ie

www.omniumsanctorumhiberniae.blogspot.ie

www.pilgrimagemediavalireland.com

www.ucc.ie/celt: Corpus of Electronic Texts (CELT). CELT is an
invaluable web resource, giving electronic access to the general
public to rare manuscripts, some of which are linked to some
of the stories here. In particular: *Annals of Ireland*; *The Life of
St Declan of Ardmore*; Geoffrey Keating's *'History of Ireland'*;
Lives of the Irish Saints; *Leabhar na Ceart (Book of Rights)*;
The Prose Tales in *The Rennes Dindshenchas*

www.shee-eire.com/Magic&Mythology

www.slieveardagh.com

www.walksireland.com

26298783R00110

Printed in Poland
by Amazon Fulfillment
Poland Sp. z o.o., Wrocław